TWO PLAYS
Alan Dent

TWO PLAYS

CRUDE

PARDON?

Alan Dent

PENNILESS PRESS PUBLICATIONS
www.pennilesspress.co.uk/books

Published by
Penniless Press Publications 2022

ISBN 978-1-913144-34-0

CONTENTS

CRUDE 7

PARDON? 128

CRUDE

A play about oil, corruption, climate change and
America.

CHARACTERS

Rich, head of Meyer Industries.
Bev, his wife.
Ted, his brother.
George, employee of Meyer.
Trig, employee of Meyer.
Simon, Meyer PR man.
Val Payne, Federal Prosecutor.
Tom Ralston, FBI agent.
Art, President of Meyer.
Ken, Meyer company lawyer.
Howard, ex-Meyer employee, fixer.
Dick, company auditor.
Sam, FBI superior.
Fred Buxton, Republican Senator.
Phil Read, attorney, US attorney's office.
Jim Close, attorney who replaces Phil Read.
Joe Brady, ex-Meyer employee.
William, native American chief.
Caroline Sweeney, girl, 17.
Pop, her father.

The play is structured so that these characters can be played by five actors (possibly four), four male (possibly three) and one female.

SCENE ONE

A living-room. Atmosphere of great wealth. This remains the background throughout the play. The foreground provides the changing scenes.

Ted, forty, business suit. Rich, forty-five, same.

Ted: You're crooks.

Rich: Businessmen, Ted.

Ted: Where'd you get the money?

Rich: We sold stuff.

Ted: Fast.

Rich: Where's your loyalty?

Ted: To?

Rich: The family.

Ted: Family's crooked.

Rich: Half a billion. You're complaining?

Ted: Not about the money.

Rich: What would pop say?

Ted: Should've told him?

Rich: What?

Ted: He was a crook.

Rich: Your own father?

Ted: You were scared of him.

Rich: I admired him.

Ted: He forced you.

Rich: No one forces me.

Ted; Why'd you come home?

Rich: The business.

Ted: He threatened to sell.

Rich: I chose.

Ted: He scared everyone. You. Mom. Us. Tom was right.

Rich: Tom is flaky.

Ted: Not a crook.

Rich: Half a billion. He's not complaining.

Ted: Shoulda stayed away.

Rich: No head for business.

Ted: He's not a crook.

Rich: What do we provide?

Ted: Dunno.

Rich: It's a responsibility, Ted.

Ted: It sure is.

Rich: Want your mobile, you need petrochemicals.

Ted: From the get-go.

Rich: He built the business from nothing.

Ted: Liar. He inherited and stole the formula.

Rich: He did not steal it.

Ted: He worked it out?

Rich: The Supreme Court...

Ted: What do they know?

Rich: That's the law, Ted.

Ted: I'm suing you.

Rich: Go ahead.

Ted: You're fraudsters.

Rich: We operate in the market.

Ted: You operate when the market breaks down.

Rich: You know what happens when things get regulated?
Look at the atmosphere, the oceans.

Ted: Yeah?

Rich: Regulated. See? That's why there's such a mess. Leave
it to the market.

Ted: Pop stole the formula.

Rich; That not what the law said.

Ted: He tweaked it.

Rich That was smart.

Ted: Crooked.

Rich: He made you wealthy.

Ted: He was right to crack crude for Stalin?

Rich: You know he was in the John Birch.

Ted: Sure. But he cracked crude for Stalin.

Rich: He hadn't, someone else would.

Ted: Let someone else.

Rich: Go outta business?

Ted: Business with communists?

Rich: He hated communists.

Ted: Sure did. Built a big refinery for Hitler.

Rich: Good business.

Ted: Yep, all that oil musta given Adolf a headstart when he invaded Poland.

Rich: You do business where you can do business. You know that.

Ted: Communists on Monday, fascists on Tuesday.

Rich: He repented.

Ted: Helping Hitler?

Rich: Lots of American companies operated in the Third Reich.

Ted: Sure. Then came Pearl Harbour.

Rich: You gotta be prosperous to have the best army.

Ted: OPEC put on the embargo, you screwed US customers.

Rich: We paid the fine.

Ted: Sure. Fines are cheaper than honesty.

Rich: We respect the law.

Ted: Like with the exploration tracts.

Rich: The government offers leases why shouldn't we bid?

Ted: You didn't bid.

Rich: We got agents.

Ted: That's fraud.

Rich: Okay. We pushed the envelope.

Ted: You set fire to the envelope.

Rich: You think this country was built by cissies?

Ted: On the corpses of the American tribes.

Rich: Savages.

Ted: They lived here.

Rich: You know how much oil there is under their land?

Ted: Tell me.

Rich: Tens of millions of dollars.

Ted: They'll be rich.

Rich: They don't know how.

Ted: They can learn.

Rich: They want to learn?

Ted: I guess.

Rich: They aren't like us.

Ted: Not crooks?

Rich: You think we shoulda left this country to savages?

Ted: Maybe they were honest.

Rich: Thousands of years, what did they do?

Ted: Hunt bison.

Rich: You think progress is a mistake?

Ted: I think you gotta do business honestly, Rich.

Rich: Okay. We break the law, we get fined. We pay the fine. That's honest.

Ted: That's buying your way out.

Rich: You want government to control business? That's McCarthyism.

Ted: You like communists?

Rich: We resist government every legal way.

Ted: Cracking units for Stalin is resisting government?

Rich: Opportunity.

Ted: Negro soviet republic.

Rich: The whites made this country great.

Ted: You made it crooked.

Rich: You gotta take risks to make a buck, Ted.

Ted: Take risks on white water.

Rich: When I was at MIT students were starting to hate this country.

Ted: Maybe they loved honesty.

Rich: Taxes on anyone who makes a buck. I'm sick of taxes.

Ted: People'll think you're crazy.

Rich: Carter isn't crazy?

Ted: I didn't vote for him.

Rich: You voting for Reagan?

Ted: Sure.

Rich: You're on our side.

Ted: Reagan isn't a crook.

Rich: He's against government.

Ted: He'll be the government.

Rich: We need a President who'll bring down the government.

Ted: People'll think you're crazy.

Rich: Government is crazy.

Ted: Government helps business.

Rich: Government destroys business.

Ted: Okay. No government. People shoot who they like.

Rich: Private guards.

Ted: They shoot who they like.

Rich: Keep the reds and the blacks down.

Ted: The GOP is not the KKK.

Rich: The GOP has to go.

Ted: They're gonna listen to you?

Rich: We'll buy 'em.

Ted: Some things you can't buy.

Rich: Like?

Ted: Honesty.

Rich: We're honest.

Ted: You're crooks.

Rich: About America.

Ted: Yeah?

Rich: Take Vietnam.

Ted: Take it.

Rich: That's the State.

Ted: That's anti-communism.

Rich: No State, no Vietnam.

Ted: Communists do what they like?

Rich: Arm the people.

Ted: They'll kill you.

Rich: Why?

Ted: For your money.

Rich: Not if we tell them.

Ted: What?

Rich: Who to kill.

Ted: Who?

Rich: Liberals, blacks, communists.

Ted: Lotta dead people.

Rich: They listen, they stay alive.

Ted: They don't have weapons?

Rich: Who?

Ted: Liberals, blacks, communists?

Rich: They don't.

Ted: They aren't the people?

Rich: The people are patriots.

Ted: Arm half the people?

Rich: Why not?

Ted: Even more dead people.

Rich: The alternative?

Ted: Honesty.

Rich: You want a black in the White House?

Ted: Never happen.

Rich: What's Reagan?

Ted: Conservative.

Rich: Front man.

Ted: Sure.

Rich: Actor.

Ted: Sure.

Rich: He delivers the lines.

Ted: Sure.

Rich: Who writes the lines?

Ted: Staffers.

Rich: We do.

Ted: The GOP is gonna let you?

Rich: The GOP understands money.

Ted: Gonna buy the voters?

Rich: Sure.

Ted (scoffs): How?

Rich: We got 'em.

Ted: How?

Rich: Papers, radio, tv.

Ted: Washington Post?

Rich: Who reads it?

Ted: Ideas spread.

Rich: You're right.

Ted: Democrats gonna stop talking?

Rich: Reagan will crush the Democrats.

Ted: Sure.

Rich: How?

Ted: Carter's no good.

Rich: We told 'em.

Ted: Who?

Rich The people.

Ted: You did?

Rich: We did. Every day.

Ted: Good.

Rich: Yeah, good. You're on our side.

Ted: Honest business.

Rich: What's honest?

Ted: Don't cheat.

Rich: What's cheating?

Ted: Play by the rules.

Rich: Who make the rules?

Ted: The people.

Rich: Liberal crap.

Ted: Democracy is crap?

Rich: Who the blacks gonna vote for?

Ted: Gotta beat 'em fair and square.

Rich; That's irresponsible.

Ted: Fight by the rules.

Rich: Give those people power, they'll destroy us.

Ted: They can't destroy us.

Rich You are so naïve.

Ted: Yeah? I'm not a crook.

Rich: We make money, they vote for the government to steal it.

Ted: You stole it.

Rich: We did not steal it.

Ted: You stole from me.

Rich: Everybody gets what they can.

Ted: If they steal it?

Rich: Human nature, Ted.

Ted: You're the biggest crooks in the business.

Rich: You want the unions to run this country?

Ted: The unions?

Rich: Public sector unions got the Democrats back.

Ted: Who cares?

Rich: Look at Wisconsin.

Ted: What about it?

Rich; They go it tied up.

Ted: The unions?

Rich: Sure?

Ted: You're crazy.

Rich: I'm crazy? Union dollars control the State.

Ted: One State.

Rich: Dominoes.

Ted: What?

Rich: One falls, then the next, then the next.

Ted: Reagan gonna lose in Wisconsin?

Rich: State power matters in a federal system.

Ted: Unions got in your way?

Rich: Unions get in everybody's way.

Ted: Vote 'em down.

Rich: Gotta cut 'em off at the knees.

Ted: How?

Rich: The law.

Ted: The law? You care about the law.

Rich: The law has to serve American prosperity, Ted.

Ted: Sure. Honest prosperity.

Rich: The measure is money.

Ted: Sure. Honest money.

Rich: Honesty never stopped a man being poor.

Ted: Being rich stops a man being honest?

Rich: You gotta do what's necessary in business, Ted.

Ted: Like pop.

Rich: Took his chance.

Ted: Stole the formula.

Rich: Maybe he did, but he got away with it.

Ted; You got away with it all right.

Rich: Court's decision.

Ted: Miscarriage.

Rich: The law has to serve…

Ted: You'll see what the law serves.

Rich: Do your worst.

Ted: Got your lawyers in line?

Rich: The best.

Ted: Half a billion. I can pay.

Rich: Throwing it away.

Ted: I got it honestly.

Rich: From us.

Ted: From you.

Rich: We're crooks?

Ted: You are.
Rich: Then what are you?

BLACKOUT

SCENE TWO

Pipeline across open country.
George fifty, plump. Trig, early twenties, athletic, quick. Both wear overalls and hard hats.

Trig: Rust.
George: Metal rusts.
Trig: Gotta be dangerous.
George: Leave it.
Trig: Could blow.
George: Blows, they'll clean up.
Trig: Rust all over.
George: Not our problem.
Trig: We maintain that thing.
George: Sure.
Trig: Paid to.
George: Sure.
Trig: We oughta do somethin'.
George: Do what we're told.
Trig: Our job.
George: Our job's make the company money.
Trig: Company be in trouble that blows.
George: Company knows.
Trig: Thank us for doin' our job.
George: Company won't thank you for costing.
Trig: How many gallons flow through that thing?
George: Thousands.
Trig: That blows there's a big clean up.
George: Company knows.
Trig: Yeah?
George: I seen it.
Trig: Yeah?
George: Bury it.

Trig: That much?

George: Get a boat, engine sends it downstream.

Trig: Gonna show up somewhere.

George: Not our problem.

Trig: Oil, that's bad.

George: That's money, boy.

Trig: I read about this guy.

George: Uh-uh.

Trig: English. Callender. He worked out the earth is warming.

George: Politics.

Trig: No. Way back.

George: Not our business.

Trig: You gotta ask yourself.

George: You gotta do what the company says.

Trig: You gotta wonder.

George: Company doesn't pay you to wonder, Trig.

Trig: We doin' here?

George: Checkin' the pipeline.

Trig: Rust everywhere.

George: Gotta keep that quiet.

Trig: That blows, who gets it?

George: We submit the report.

Trig: Rust everywhere.

George: Can't say that. Cost the company.

Trig: Say what?

George: Everything's fine.

Trig: It blows?

George: Company's got the report.

Trig: The report is lies.

George: Report is what we're paid to say.

Trig: We gotta tell the truth, George.

George: Ain't paid to tell the truth.

Trig: So it blows.

George: Sure.

Trig: Thousands o' gallons.

George: Sure.

Trig: Who's responsible?

George: Shit happens.

Trig: You seen that thing?

George: Things wear out, Trig.

Trig: We could stop it.

George: How?

Trig: Tell the company.

George: Tell the company what?

Trig: Pipeline's rust.

George: Company wanna hear that?

Trig: Company wanna hear the truth?

George: Company wanna make money, boy.

Trig: You gotta ask yourself.

George: You want your bonus?

Trig: Sure.

George: Make the company money.

Trig: I dunno.

George: You don't want your bonus?

Trig: Sure.

George: Kid on the way.

Trig: Yeah.

George: Need the money.

Trig: Sure.

George: Create value.

Trig: Gotta be repaired some time.

George: Not our business.

Trig: Blows, that's a lotta oil gone.

George: If it works, don't fix it.

Trig: Ain't gonna work long.

George: Rust holds.

Trig: Yeah?

George: I seen it.

Trig: Yeah?

George: Sure. That pipe might be good for three months.

Trig: Three months?

George: Lotta oil.

Trig: What then?

George: Lotta value.

Trig: Three months?

George: We get our bonus.

Trig: It blows.

George: Sure.

Trig: That's crazy.

George: Not our business.

Trig: Gonna cost the company.

George: Patch it up.

Trig: Laws.

George: They got lawyers.

Trig: Someone checks that pipeline.

George: We checked it.

Trig: We gotta say.

George: We send the report.

Trig: It's lies.

George: Company's got lawyers.

Trig: Government's got lawyers.

George: Government likes business.

Trig: Sure.

George: What we get paid for.

Trig: Company wants a good reputation.

George: Reputation don't pay the bills.

Trig: We get paid to look after the pipeline.

George: Your pay's an advance, boy.

Trig: Advance?

George: You create value, the company compensates you.

Trig: Sure.

George: That's your pay.

Trig: Bonus.

George: Nope. Advance.

Trig: They gotta pay us.

George: Only if we create value.

Trig: We fix the pipe, that's value.

George: How d'we fix it?

Trig: Shut it down.

George: Cost a lotta money.

Trig: Don't shut down the pipe, you can't fix it.

George: Don't shut down the pipe, you make money.

Trig: Three months.

George: Yeah.

Trig: Then?

George: See what happens.

Trig: We know.

George: We got an idea.

Trig: Could be a big spill.

George: Sure. Could be small.

Trig: We can stop that.

George: Want your bonus?

Trig: Who cares?

George: I got bills.

Trig: Everyone got bills, George.

George: Company makes the rules.

Trig: Somebody dies?

George: Lawyers' business.

Trig: Our business.

George: We do the job.

Trig: We gotta say. In the report.

George: Company doesn't wanna hear that.

Trig: Our responsibility.

George: Say what?

Trig: That pipeline's done.

George: Company gonna take that?

Trig: We do the check.

George: Company wants proof.

Trig: Proof.

George: Sure.

Trig: Of?

George: Pipeline's okay.

Trig: Okay? Useless, George.

George: They got proof, they're saved.

Trig: Us?

George: 'Cares about us?

Trig: Somebody dies, George. We lied.

George: Who knows?

Trig: They send experts.

George: Goes to court. The lawyers nail it.

Trig: We know.

George: We did our job.

Trig: We didn't.

George: Who pays us?

Trig: Yeah, but.

George: But?

Trig: Somebody dies, I'm responsible.

George: Company's responsible.

Trig: I'm not the company.

George: Company buys you.

Trig: My mind.

George: You sold it.

Trig: I dunno, George.

George: Quit worrying. We get our bonus.

Trig: What you gonna say?

George: Wanna read it?

Trig: Sure.

George gives him report. Trig reads.

George: You just gotta tick boxes.

Trig: This ain't right, George.

George: Too late.

Trig: You stand by that in court?

George: Sure.

Trig: Somebody dies, you stand by that?

George: Sure.

Trig: I dunno.

George: Company'll look after us.

Trig: Company been in a lotta trouble.

George: Still makes money.

Trig: One day.

George: One day?

Trig: They come after someone, could be us.

George: We done anything wrong?

Trig: This.

George: The old man got influence.

Trig: I know.

George: Reagan.

Trig: Bush?

George: Sure. Oil man.

Trig: But this.

George: Take it easy.

Trig: You gonna submit that?

George: What else?

Trig: Maybe change a few things.

George: You think?

Trig: Look here. You could change that.

George (put on his glasses): That?

Trig: Yeah. That's not too bad.

George: Look bad in court.

Trig: Not our responsibility.

George: You gotta understand, Trig.

Trig: I get it.

George: This is business. We don't get involved.

Trig: We aren't involved?

George: We work.

Trig: Sure. We fix the pipe.

George: When it's broke.

Trig: It's rust, George.

George: You see any leaks?

Trig; Want me to show ya?

George: What?

Trig: One blow with this wrench.

George: Don't do that, boy.

Trig: You know.

George: Criminal damage.

Trig: Doin' my job.

George: Leave it be.

Trig: One blow, we're up to our knees.

George: Lose your job.

Trig: Can't be right.

George: This is a great country.

Trig: Sure.

George: Business made it great.

Trig Sure.

George: Don't interfere with that.

Trig: Interfere?

George: The old man makes billions, we keep our jobs.

Trig: He can pay.

George: He decides.

Trig: Our job.

George: No.

Trig: No?

George: The report is our job.

Trig: We make a little hole.

George: You crazy.

Trig: A trickle.

George shakes his head.

Trig: Report it.

George: Company wants to hear that?

Trig: A drop.

George: Don't do it.

Trig: My finger.

George: No, Trig.

Trig: See that?

George: What?

Trig: Gives.

George: Don't jab it.

Trig: Three months?

George: Sure.

Trig: Three weeks. Three hours.

George: I seen pipes like that last.

Trig: Ever see one blow?

George: Sure.

Trig: Mess?

George: Sure.

Trig: Not right, George.

George: Right? I gotta get paid.

Trig: This guy.

George: What guy?

Trig: Callender.

George: Forget him.

Trig: He worked it out.

George: He's right?

Trig: I think.

George: He got the proof?

Trig; Yeah.

George: So what?

Trig: So we gotta stop it?

George: Who?

Trig: Us

George: You and me?

Trig: Sure.

George: Leave it to the big guys.

Trig: Government.

George: Company.

Trig: Company lets it rust.

George: They'll work it out.

Trig: Three months?

George: Give 'em time.

Trig: We got time?

George: Enough.

Trig: Dunno.

George: How'd the old man get rich?

Trig: Business.

George: You got it.

Trig: Business doing the damage, George.

George: They got it worked out.

Trig: Bit of pipeline.

George: Lot of oil.

Trig: Coupla weeks.

George: Not our money.

Trig: Pipe like that in your house, you gonna wait?

George: They got rights?

Trig: Rights?

George: They pay.

Trig: The land.

George: Clean it up.

Trig: I dunno.

George: You worry too much.

Trig: That blows. Somebody dies.

George: People die every day.

Trig: Think that's fit?

George: For what?

Trig: Oil.

George: Ain't broke.

Trig: Yet.

George: Company says, it ain't broke don't fix it.

Trig: One tap with this wrench.

George: Crime, Trig.

Trig: Who's gonna know?

George: Us.

Trig: Say nothin'.

George: They'll know.

Trig: How?

George: Experts.

Trig: Wanna leave it?

George: Leave it.

Trig: What we here for?

George: Report.

Trig: We gotta change it.

George: Ain't changin' nothin'.

Trig: One tap.

George: Don't.

Trig: We gonna leave it?

George: We are.

Trig: Why?

George: Bonus.

Trig: That's it?

George: That's it.

BLACKOUT

SCENE THREE

As scene one.

Rich on sofa and landline. Bev beside him looking at *Cosmopolitan*. Simon's voice heard on landline.

Rich: Our ideas.

Simon: Everywhere.

Rich: The politicians?

Simon: All of 'em.

Rich: Not enough.

Simon: No?

Rich: Intellectuals.

Simon: We got 'em.

Rich: Not enough.

Simon: Good people.

Rich: I know.

Simon: Philosophers, economists, sociologists, literary critics.

Rich: On the ground.

Simon: We are.

Rich: Our propositions.

Simon: Getting through.

Rich: Unanswerable.

Simon: Sure.

Bev leans to Rich, shows him a page. He nods. She makes a coy face and laughs.

Rich: When we say capitalism, they say capitalism.

Simon: What else?

Rich: What's a man live for, Simon?

Simon: Tell me?

Rich: His own well-being.

Simon: That's freedom.

Rich: That's capitalism.

Simon: Right.

Rich: Look after the other guy?

Simon: Look after himself.

Rich: Rational.

Simon: It is.

Rich: Emotion all over the place.

Simon: Atlas.

Rich: I shrug, the world falls.

Simon: It does.

Rich: Who reads Ayn Rand?

Simon: Our people.

Rich: Philosophers?

Simon: Who cares?

Rich: Professors teach our kids.

Simon: Gotta buy 'em.

Rich: Liberals all over the place.

Simon: Irrational.

Rich: No logic.

Simon: Right.

Rich: They think?

Simon: They do not.

Rich: Touchy-feely stuff.

Simon: Flaky.

Rich: Reason is absolute.

Simon: Rules the world.

Rich: They know that?

Simon: They do not.

Rich: They're teaching our kids, Simon.

Simon: They can be bought.

Rich: Gotta be everywhere.

Simon: We are.

Rich: Networks.

Simon: We got 'em.

Rich: Not enough.

Simon: True.

Rich: Where's liberty?

Simon: You're right.

Rich: Keynes is everywhere.

Simon: Gotta kill it.

Rich: That's communism.

Simon: More or less.

Rich: More or less?

Simon: Minor differences.

Rich: Minor?

Simon: Minimal.

Rich: Logic?

Simon: No logic.

Rich: Right. Emotion.

Simon: Irrational.

Rich: Did emotion make me rich?

Simon: It did not.

Rich: Reason.

Simon: Absolutely.

Rich: Who thinks?

Simon: We do.

Rich: The people think?

Simon: They do not.

Rich: The people feel.

Simon: They do.

Rich: Like animals.

Simon: They know nothing.

Rich: They should know?

Simon: They should not.

Rich: The people start interfering, what then?

Simon: Chaos.

Rich: What's in their heads?

Simon: Nothing.

Rich: Our ideas?

Simon: Doin' it.

Rich: There's truth.

Simon: There is.

Rich: Truth is absolute.

Simon: Sure.

Rich: Morality is absolute.

Simon: Damn right.

Rich: The people got morality?

Simon: They do not.

Rich: What's moral?

Simon: Business.

Rich: Liberals are moral?

Simon: They are not.

Rich: Unions?

Simon: Tcha.

Rich: Tryin' to shut me down.

Bev gets up and adjusts her hair before the mirror. Gestures to Rich, "like it?" He nods. She sits down and picks up the magazine.

Simon: Legislate.

Rich: Correct.

Simon: We got the power.

Rich: Reagan.

Simon: Sure.

Rich: He'll do it.

Simon: He will.

Rich: Thatcher.

Simon: She'll do it.

Rich: Altrusim.

Simon: Dangerous.

Rich: Fatal.

Simon: To business.

Rich: To liberty.

Simon: Kills it.

Rich: She's against it.

Simon: Implacably.

Rich: Rational ethics.

Simon: The market.

Rich: Freedom.

Simon: The individual.

Rich: She'll close the NHS?

Simon: She will.

Rich: That's communism.

Simon: Tyranny.

Rich: Where's the morality?

Simon: None.

Rich: What's morality?

Simon: Look after yourself.

Rich: That's logic.

Simon: Absolutely.

Rich: Absolute.

Bev folds back the pages of the magazine and puts it on Rich's lap. He looks down at the page. She smiles and nods. He nods. She takes back the magazine. Licks her finger. Flicks the pages.

Simon: Eternal.

Rich: Environmentalists on our back.

Simon: Crazies.

Rich: Know how to run a business?

Simon: No idea.

Rich: Government this, government that.

Simon: Communism.

Rich: Shut 'em down.

Simon: We can.

Rich: Our people in power.

Simon: State on our side.

Rich: First thing is ideas.

Simon: ' Course.

Rich: Universities.

Simon: Liberals everywhere.

Rich: Anarchists.
Simon: Tcha.
Rich: Papers.
Simon: Easy.
Rich: TV.
Simon: No trouble.
Rich: Schools.
Simon: Our people.
Rich: Gotta control.
Simon: Absolutely.
Rich: That's liberty.
Simon: Right.
Rich: Think tanks.
Simon: Everywhere.
Rich: Respectable.
Simon: Professors, economists, historians…
Rich: They think.
Simon: They do.
Rich: For the people.
Simon: For liberty.
Rich: Rationality.
Simon: You bet.
Rich: Masses are irrational.
Simon: Everybody knows.
Rich: Collectives think?
Simon: They do not.
Rich: Individuals think.
Simon: They do.
Rich: About?
Simon: Their advantage.
Rich: Exactly.
Simon: Human nature.
Rich: Adam Smith.
Simon: He knew.

Rich: Butcher, brewer, baker.
Simon: So right.
Rich: Group rights?
Simon: Groups have no rights.
Rich: Tyranny.
Simon: Communism.
Rich: The State.
Simon: Off our backs.
Rich: What's government for?
Simon: Tell me?
Rich: Protect business.
Simon: Correct.
Rich: Is business liberty?
Simon: It is.
Rich: Entrepreneurs.
Simon: Individuals.
Rich: My corporation.
Simon: Gotta be protected.
Rich: Else the collectives take over.
Simon: They're waiting.
Rich: Every man for himself.
Simon: That's the market.
Rich: That's liberty.
Simon: That's America.
Rich: Our wealth.
Simon: We made it.
Rich: Spread it around what happens?
Simon: Communism.
Rich: Waste.
Simon: Squandered.
Rich: The people know how to spend money?
Simon: They do not.
Rich: Throw it away.
Simon: They do.

Rich: Why are the poor poor?

Simon: No head for business.

Rich: They understand money?

Simon: They do not.

Rich: Money is rational.

Simon: Purely.

Rich: You gotta think.

Simon: Calculate.

Rich: Right.

Simon: Hard headed.

Rich: Where's sentiment get you?

Simon: Communism.

Rich: Welfare.

Simon: Money is welfare.

Rich: The market.

Simon: Nothing else.

Bev has finished the magazine, twice. She gets up. Fixes her hair in the mirror. Smooths her skirt. Looks at her watch. Sits down. Hooks one leg over the other. Rocks it. Looks at Rich. Picks up the magazine. Licks her finger. Flicks the pages. Stops. Folds back the spine. Shows Rich a page. He raises his eyebrows. Nods. She giggles. Licks her finger. Flicks the pages.

Rich: Did Smith say that?

Simon: He did?

Rich: Invisible hand.

Simon: Everywhere.

Rich: Intervene what happens?

Simon: Communism.

Rich: Things go haywire.

Simon: They do.

Rich: Cutting off the invisible hand.

Simon: Feeds you.

Rich: The people know that?

Simon: They do not.

Rich: Gotta get our message out.

Simon: We're on it.

Rich: Mont Pelerin.

Simon: Got 'em.

Rich: This guy Hansen.

Simon: Shut him up.

Rich: If he's right.

Simon: Right?

Rich: Maybe.

Simon: Maybe I'm a crocodile.

Rich: Science may be right.

Simon: Yeah, but..

Rich: The answer?

Simon: That's it.

Rich: Leave it to us.

Simon: Who else?

Rich: Governments start meddling, what you got?

Simon: Communism.

Rich: Business knows.

Simon: Naturally.

Rich: These scientists.

Simon: Yeah?

Rich: Who's on our side?

Simon: Not business people.

Rich: That's the issue.

Simon: It is.

Rich: Scientists know how to run an oil business?

Simon: They do not.

Rich: Adam Smith a scientist?

Simon: He was not.

Rich: Hayek a scientist?

Simon: He was not.

Rich: Guy may be right.

Simon: Possible.

Rich: Not about the solution.

Simon: Business is the solution.

Rich: Scientists get active what you get?

Simon: Communism.

Rich: The market knows.

Simon: Always.

Rich: We serve the people.

Simon: They complain?

Rich: They do not.

Simon: Unless propaganda.

Rich: Unless. Give 'em what they want.

Simon: That's business.

Rich: They wanna live in caves?

Simon: They do not.

Rich: They want cars?

Simon: They do.

Rich: They want planes?

Simon: They do.

Rich: That's democracy.

Simon: The people decide.

Rich: The people know.

Simon: They do.

Rich: Consumers know.

Simon: Can't fault 'em.

Rich: This guy, these guys, want treaties.

Simon: Government to government.

Rich: What's that get you?

Simon: Communism.

Rich: Consumers want oil?

Simon: Gotta have it.

Rich: They want low prices.

Simon: Rational.

Rich: The point.

Simon: The market.

Rich: Serves consumers.

Simon: It does.

Rich: Treaties, what happens?

Simon: Prices (he makes an upwards gesture with his stiff forefinger).

Rich: What built this country?

Simon: Free enterprise.

Rich: Cheap oil.

Simon: Lifeblood.

Rich: These guys want cheap oil?

Simon: Communists.

Rich: Planet warming, who's gonna save it?

Simon: Entrepreneurs.

Rich: Scientists get that?

Simon: Make 'em.

Rich: You gotta get to those guys, Simon.

Bev gets up. Fixes her hair. Picks up the magazine. Licks her finger. Flicks the pages, shows one to Rich. Nods. He nods. She stays on her feet flicking through the pages and stopping for a few seconds to check her hair in the mirror.

Simon: We got 'em.

Rich: People get the wrong idea.

Simon: Liberals all over the place.

Rich: Government this, government that.

Simon: Communism.

Rich: Planet warming.

Simon: You think?

Rich: Sure.

Simon: Nature. Who's to say?

Rich: We deny it, scientists'll have us.

Simon: We shut 'em up.

Rich: Gotta get the message out. Business will solve it.

Simon: Solves everything.

Rich: Find the means.

Simon: Always.

Rich: Stop burning oil, that's a sick idea.

Simon: Communism.

Rich: Skin in the game.

Simon: Lotta skin.

Rich: Our ideas.

Simon: We're on it.

Rich: Our people.

Simon: Everywhere.

Rich: Congress.

Simon: Buy 'em.

Rich: They listen to Hansen.

Simon: Shut him up.

Rich: Get him on our side, Simon.

Bev (facing him): Rich?

Rich: Uh-uh?

BLACKOUT

SCENE FOUR

An office. Woman attorney, on phone.

Val: Hi, Tom.

Tom: Big.

Val: You think?

Tom: Pictures.

Val: Yeah.

Tom: See me, hidin' behind cows.

She laughs.

Val: Professional, Tom.

Tom: We got 'em.

Val: Won't lie down.

Tom: Knock 'em down.

Val: I dunno.

Tom: Gotta take it, Val.

Val: Need more than newspaper reports.

Tom: Got it.

Val: Well, you think.

Tom: Behind bars.

Val: The little guys.

Tom: Right to the top, Val.

Val: Hidin' behind cows ?

Tom: Orders.

Val: Prove it?

Tom: Federal Grand Jury.

Val: I dunno, Tom.

Tom: Move fast.

Val: They gonna stand still?

Tom: They got money, we got the law.

Val: You know those guys.

Tom: Sure.

Val: Sacrifice the underlings.

Tom: They'll testify.

Val: You think?

Tom: Doin' their job.

Val: Theft?

Tom: Or fired.

Val: Law's the law.

Tom: Documents.

Val: Got 'em?

Tom: Not yet.

Val: Ever?

Tom: How it works.

Val: Yeah?

Tom; From the top.

Val: Cover their tracks.

Tom: Senate's investigating.

Val: They buy power.

Tom: Not us.

Val: Sure.

Tom: Docs are falsified.

Val: Got any?

Tom: Photos.

Val: Of docs?

Tom: Of employees.

Val: Long way to go, Tom.

Tom: Is this America?

Val: Sure.

Tom: Is this the rule of law?

Val: Sure.

Tom: Is this the little guy's country?

Val: Sure.

Tom: Big guys been stealin' from little guys.

Val: Big guys got money.

Tom: You side with money?

Val: I got to ask.

Tom: What?

Val: We gonna nail 'em?

Tom; To the floor.

Val: Big guys?

Tom: Absolutely.

Val: Okay, Tom.

Tom: Empower that jury.

Val: Sure.

Tom: Gotta move fast.

Val: The law move fast?

Tom: Fast as we can. Get the big man behind bars.

Val: Fast as we can, Tom.

BLACKOUT

SCENE FIVE

An office. Rich behind desk, Art opposite.

Rich: Let's see.

Art hands over paper.

Art: Done.

Rich (reading): Who got this?

Art: Everyone.

Rich: Everyone?

Art: You bet.

Rich: That wise?

Art: Sure.

Rich: You think.

Art: Destroyed.

Rich: Everything?

Art: Every scrap.

Rich: Suppose.

Art: Yeah?

Rich: Someone doesn't.

Art: They will.

Rich: Just one.

Art: They wanna eat?

Rich: I know.

Art: Burnt, shredded, gone.

Rich: Follow up.

Art: Sure.

Rich (quoting): "Useful to competitors".

Art: Everything.

Rich: Open to interpretation?

Art: No. Everything.

Rich: Senate investigation?

Art: They know?

Rich: Been in the papers.

Art: One.

Rich: The rest?

Art: Shut 'em up.

Rich: One bad document, I'm in prison.

Art: Won't happen.

Rich: Sure?

Art: Don't even think.

Rich: Some guager?

Art: Daren't.

Rich: In a pocket. Taken home.

Art: Tight control.

Rich: They blab.

Art: They wanna work?

Rich: Without mismeasurement, I'm clear.

Art: Evidence?

Rich: All of it?

Art; Gone.

Rich: I go down, you too.

Art: Sure, Rich.

BLACKOUT

SCENE SIX

Same office. Rich on phone.

Ken: Texas.

Rich: What's he say?

Ken: Told to destroy written evaluations.

Rich: That's bad?

Ken: Need the records.

Rich: All?

Ken: Sure.

Rich: Gone, Ken.

Ken: Gone?

Rich: Shredded, burnt.

Ken: Bad idea.

Rich: You think?

Ken: Companies keep records.

Rich: False records?

Ken: They know they're false?

Rich: Work it out?

Ken: How?

Rich; Obvious.

Ken: A little modification.

Rich: They're gone, Ken.

Ken: When?

Rich: Dunno. Art sent a memo.

Ken: Call it back.

Rich: Too late.

Ken: Try.

Rich: Okay. This guy in Texas.

Ken: Yeah.

Rich: Gonna disappear?

Ken: Disappear, Rich?

Rich: He talks.

Ken: Need the records.

Rich: Or?

Ken: Look pretty strange.

Rich: The guy talks.

Ken: Evidence, Rich.

Rich: One guy in Texas. That's prison.

Ken: Calm down.

Rich: Pay him off.

Ken: I'm a lawyer, Rich.

Rich: My lawyer.

Ken: Sure.

Rich: I'll pay him off.

Ken: Better keep the records.

Rich: See what I can do.

Ken: Okay.

Rich: Just one guy in Texas?

Ken: Just one.

BLACKOUT

SCENE SEVEN

As scene one. Rich on sofa , relaxed. Howard beside him.

Rich: Look well.
Howard: Fine. You?
Rich: Never better. Golf?
Howard: Every day.
Rich: The life.
Howard: Worked for it.
Rich: Both.
Howard: Anyway?
Rich: Federal Grand Jury.
Howard: What they got?
Rich: Guy in Texas.
Howard: One guy?
Rich: FBI. Everywhere.
Howard: FBI ?
Rich: Straight guy.
Howard: Buy him off.
Rich shakes his head.
Howard: No? Get him moved.
Rich: Employees talk?
Howard: First job.
Rich: Yeah?
Howard: Get 'em on your side.
Rich: Buy 'em?
Howard: You pay 'em.
Rich: Okay.
Howard: Already bought.
Rich: Yeah. But they talk.
Howard: Make connections.
Rich: You think.
Howard: Everybody has a past.

Rich: Dig it up?

Howard: Sure. Where's the weight?

Rich: Thousands.

Howard: They all talk?

Rich: Who knows?

Howard: They don't, where's the case?

Rich: Documents.

Howard: Destroy 'em.

Rich: Lawyer says keep 'em.

Howard: Some.

Rich: No complaint, no crime?

Howard: Got it.

Rich: How?

Howard: Ways and means.

Rich: You do it?

Howard: Love to.

Rich: Worked for us how long?

Howard: Thirteen.

Rich: Know the company.

Howard: Inside out.

Rich: Honest?

Howard: Utterly honorable.

Rich: Contacts?

Howard: Business, Wall St, Washington.

Rich: Employees say nothing, company's straight. Where's the case?

Howard: Exactly.

Rich: Ten million a year.

Howard: Yeah?

Rich: We stole it.

Howard: Extracted it.

Rich: Stole it.

Howard: From redskins?

Rich: Their land.

Howard: Sitting on billions.
Rich: Trained the guagers.
Howard: Yeah?
Rich: Take this much, say that much.
Howard: That's business.
Rich: Government is anti-business.
Howard: Sure.
Rich: Gotta shut it down, Howard.
Howard: Government?
Rich: I'm learning.
Howard: We pull the strings.
Rich: Judicial system is anti-business.
Howard: We got judges.
Rich: Judges read Hayek?
Howard: Some.
Rich: Law has to be interpreted.
Howard: Right.
Rich: In favour of business.
Howard: What else?
Rich: Communism.
Howard: Right.
Rich: I'm starting to see.
Howard: Yeah?
Rich: Government is the enemy.
Howard: Democrats.
Rich: Republicans any better?
Howard: Well…
Rich: Gotta save this country, Howard.
Howard: I know.
Rich: People gotta rise up for freedom.
Howard: Country's built on it.
Rich: What's freedom?
Howard: The individual.
Rich: Business.

Howard: The American way.

Rich: Government gotta be pro-business.

Howard: People want it.

Rich: People are duped.

Howard: Sure.

Rich: Martin Luther King.

Howard: Oh yeah.

Rich: The man was a communist.

Howard: Demagogue.

Rich: Liberals everywhere.

Howard: Ruin this country.

Rich: So I stole a little oil.

Howard: Purloined.

Rich: From redskins.

Howard: They use it?

Rich: For that I'm a criminal?

Howard: An honorable man.

Rich: What I've done for this country.

Howard: Work you give people.

Rich: Strong government.

Howard: Gotta have it.

Rich: Protect business.

Howard: What else?

Rich: Bush?

Howard: Okay.

Rich: Too weak.

Howard: You think?

Rich: Liberals, unions..

Howard: I guess.

Rich: Gotta change the system.

Howard: In our favour.

Rich: People vote. Chaos.

Howard: Well..

Rich: They gotta be educated.

Howard: Sure.

Rich: They read Hayek?

Howard: Funny papers.

Rich: I'm learning.

Howard: Sure.

Rich: Keep me outa prison, okay.

Howard: No question.

Rich: But we use this.

Howard: We do.

Rich: We organise.

Howard: Democracy.

Rich: Save this country.

Howard: Absolutely.

BLACKOUT

SCENE EIGHT

Native American reservation. Atmosphere of modest means.
William, tribal chief sits opposite Dick, accountant.

Dick: Team on this.
William: Grateful.
Dick: Got accountants?
William: No.
Dick: Twelve auditors.
William: Very grateful.
Dick: Skilled.
William: ' Course.
Dick: Highly trained.
William: Good.
Dick: Head for figures?
William: No.
Dick: Hard math.
William: Yes.
Dick: Look here (shows him a paper).
William: Yes.
Dick: Get it?
William: Not sure.
Dick: This. Look there.
William: What's it mean?
Dick: You gotta subtract the differential from the coefficient.
William: You do?
Dick: To get the denominator.
William: Yeah.
Dick: Know what the denominator is?
William: Like in fractions?
Dick: Fractions. Good. (takes back paper). Expert work.
William: Very grateful.
Dick: Numbers don't lie.

William: No.

Dick: That's fact (waves paper).

William: Sure.

Dick: What I'm seein' here.

William: They stole our oil?

Dick: You think so?

William: They did.

Dick: You got figures?

William: No.

Dick: You got auditors?

William: No.

Dick: Experts?

William: No.

Dick: Amateurs do this?

William: Dunno.

Dick: Twelve auditors.

William: Grateful.

Dick: Harvard. Princeton. Brains (taps his temple).

William: Good.

Dick: What I'm seeing here.

William: Our oil?

Dick: Figures.

William: Yes.

Dick: Truth.

William: Yes.

Dick (shaking his head): Equations.

William: Yeah?

Dick: Quadratics.

William: Yeah?

Dick: Know quadratics?

William shakes his head.

Dick: All about quadratics.

William: It is?

Dick: Calculus.

William: Yeah?

Dick: Heard o'calculus?

William shakes his head.

Dick: Brains (taps his temple). What I'm seein' here.

William: Five years.

Dick: Huh ?

William: Stole our oil.

Dick: Evidence?

William: We know.

Dick: We know this, we know that. World runs on evidence.

William: Told us.

Dick: Who?

William: Guagers.

Dick: Those guys?

William: Good men.

Dick: Know calculus?

William: Dunno.

Dick: Educated?

William: High school.

Dick: Princeton? Harvard? MIT?

William: Dunno.

Dick: Figures (taps his temple).

William: Sure.

Dick: Brains.

William: I know.

Dick: What I'm seeing here.

William: Yeah?

Dick: Figures don't lie.

William: No.

Dick: Look at that? (shoves paper under William's nose then withdraws it fast)

William: What?

Dick: Big number.

William: Sure.

Dick: We call it, conversion factor.

William: You do?

Dick: Meaning?

William: Dunno.

Dick: You owe us twenty thousand dollars.

William: How?

Dick: Been stealing.

William: Stealing?

Dick: Falsifying.

William: How?

Dick: Take this much, say that much.

William: No.

Dick: Twelve auditors.

William: Don't cheat.

Dick: Figures, William.

William: We're honest people.

Dick: Tell the judge.

William: Judge?

Dick: Fraud.

William: No.

Dick (waves paper): Proof.

William: They took our oil.

Dick: Figures?

William: We know.

Dick: Evidence, William.

William: Twenty thousand?

Dick: Bureau of Indian Affairs hears about this.

William: Don't have it.

Dick: Spent it?

William: Honest people.

Dick: You say.

William: Our culture.

Dick: Culture this, culture that.

William: Can't pay.

Dick: Suppose.

William: What?

Dick: Our mistake. We overpaid.

William: You did?

Dick: Say.

William: Your figures?

Dick: Mistakes happen.

William: We didn't steal.

Dick: Got it.

William: We'd know.

Dick: You didn't.

William: We didn't?

Dick: Hundred here, hundred there. Adds up.

William: Mistake.

Dick: Sure.

William: Yours.

Dick: Why not?

William: So?

Dick: Forget your stolen oil, we say nothing.

William: They owe us millions.

Dick: What's the judge say?

William: Truth.

Dick: Evidence (he waves the papers).

William: Honest people.

Dick: Sure. Our mistake.

William: Okay.

BLACKOUT

SCENE NINE

Office. Rich on mobile opposite Howard.

Howard: Public.
Rich: Yeah?
Howard: Their newspaper. Nation News, whatever.
Rich (into mobile): Public statement, Simon.
Simon: Yeah.
Rich : What he say?
Howard: No theft.
Rich (into mobile): No theft, Simon.
Simon: Got 'em.
Rich: Mistake?
Howard: Said nothing. No theft. That's it.
Rich (into mobile): Hear that?
Simon: Good job.
Rich: Media?
Howard: No problem.
Rich: Everywhere?
Howard: Starting.
Rich: Get it everywhere.
Howard: Sure.
Rich (into mobile): Everywhere, Simon.
Simon: On it.
Rich (into mobile): Ken?
Simon: I'll tell him.
Howard: Sub-committee means nothing.
Rich: False allegations.
Howard: They are.
Rich (into mobile): Government gonna look?
Simon: Over-zealous.
Howard: Communist.
Rich: Use this.

Simon: Sure.

Rich; Save this country.

Howard: Tea party.

Rich: Popular insurgency.

Simon: Washington looks bad.

Howard: Gotta get the judges.

Rich (into mobile); Hear that, Simon.

Simon: Sure. No panic.

Howard: Senators challenge their own committee. Courts gonna fight back.

Rich (into mobile): You think, Simon?

Simon: Some.

Howard: Got an idea.

Rich: Shoot.

Howard: Campaign for judicial excellence. Big gatherings. Give 'em gradings. Let the liberals know we're onto 'em.

Rich: Simon?

Simon: Sure.

Howard: Treat 'em. Ski resorts, beachfronts. But let 'em know we're gonna publicize.

Rich: How?

Simon: Editors, pundits, commentators.

Rich: Howard?

Howard: That's it. Scare 'em and their bosses.

Rich: Attack the junk science.

Howard: Sure.

Simon: Left-wing hoax.

Rich: Right.

Howard: Courts kick it out.

Simon: Every time.

Rich: How much you need?

BLACKOUT

SCENE TEN

Office. Tom and Val.

Val: Sixty.
Tom: Yeah?
Val: This rate they'll do thousands?
Tom: Who's payin'?
Val: You think?
Tom: Story's in the Senate record.
Val: I know.
Tom: Rushin'.
Val: You bet.
Tom: No one but us.
Val: Know what they're tellin' 'em?
Tom: Earth is flat?
Val: Hayek and von Mises.
Tom: Law's the law.
Val: Sure. Don't agree with Hayek, bottom of the list.
Tom: Removed?
Val: Next step.
Tom: Gotta beat 'em.
Val: You got?
Tom: Records, right to the top.
Val: Yeah.
Tom: Exist.
Val: Got 'em?
Tom shakes his head.
Val: So?
Tom: You gotta demand.
Val: I do?
Tom: Got the power.
Val: Sure?
Tom: Sure.

Val: How?

Tom: Employees, ex-employees.

Val: Trust 'em?

Tom: Sure.

Val: Okay.

Tom: They got copies.

Val: You know?

Tom: I know.

Val: Say no.

Tom: For sure. Lost. Destroyed. But they got copies.

Val: Okay.

Tom: Fast.

Val: I'm runnin'.

BLACKOUT

SCENE ELEVEN

As scene one. Bev on sofa next to Rich, reading papers. Ken in armchair.

Ken: Okay?

Bev: Fine. You?

Ken: Top o' the world.

Bev: This about?

Ken: Aw, trivial stuff.

Bev: Got him worried.

Ken: You think.

Bev: Not sleepin'.

Ken: Men get older.

Bev: Want to get away.

Ken: Yeah?

Bev: Europe.

Ken: Sweet.

Bev: This be over soon?

Rich: All of 'em?

Ken: All.

Rich: Send 'em?

Ken (shakes head): Finished.

Rich: Her power?

Ken: Well…

Rich: Force us?

Ken: Hand over ashes?

Rich: Burnt 'em?

Ken: Not yet.

Bev picks up a magazine. Licks her finger. Flicks pages.

Rich: Said keep 'em.

Ken: Things get lost.

Rich: Lost?

Ken: Sure.

Rich; Keep 'em?

Ken: Destroy 'em, say they're lost.

Rich: Gotta right to destroy 'em?

Ken: No.

Rich: Our papers.

Ken: Law.

Rich: Can't destroy 'em?

Ken: Legally.

Rich: Lose 'em legally.

Ken: Who's to blame?

Rich: Destroy em accidentally.

Ken: Sure.

Rich: Who's to blame?

Ken: Right.

Rich: Backup copies.

Ken: Same.

Rich: Gonna believe that?

Ken: 'Cares what they believe?

Rich: Someone goes to jail?

Ken: Who's to blame?

Rich: Accident.

Ken: Right.

Rich: Some accident.

Ken: Our word.

Rich: No one goes to jail?

Ken: What they got?

Rich: FBI?

Ken: They do?

Rich: Subpoena this, subpoena that.

Ken: Subpeona ashes?

Rich: Agents seizing computers.

Ken: No right.

Rich: FBI has no right?

Ken: Judges on our side.

Rich: How many?

Ken: Sixty a time. Thousands already.

Rich: Play ball?

Ken: People like wealth.

Rich: They're right.

Ken: Wealth is virtue.

Rich: Judges think?

Ken: Virtue trumps law.

Rich: Sure.

Ken: Everyone loves virtue.

Rich: God's creation.

Ken: Wealth is virtue, virtue rules. Wealth rules.

Rich: Accident?

Ken: Simple.

Rich: Okay.

BLACKOUT

Office. Val and Tom. Tom on his feet.

Tom: Don't believe it.
Val: All gone.
Tom: Accident?
Val: They say?
Tom: You think?
Val: Liars.
Tom: Seen 'em?
Val: Uh-uh.
Tom: Read 'em?
Val: Sure.
Tom: Remember 'em?
Val: Yeah.
Tom: So?
Val: Can't.
Tom: Why not?
Val: Grand Jury secrecy.
Tom: Kiddin'?
Val: No.
Tom: Backups. I know it.
Val: For sure.
Tom: See?
She hands him a letter.
Tom: Liars.
Val: Qualified.
Tom: Do that?
Val: Lucrative.
Tom: You remember?
Val: Instructions.
Tom: From the top.
Val: Uh-uh.

Tom: From him.

Val: Himself.

Tom: Said?

Val: Measure for the company.

Tom: Take this, say that.

Val: Millions.

Tom: This is America.

Val: It is.

Tom: America built on theft, Val?

Val looks at him.

Tom: Grab their computers?

Val: Grand Jury won't allow.

Tom: I enforce the law?

Val: Your job.

Tom: My life.

Val: Mine.

Tom: Cut me off.

Val: They have.

Tom: At the knees.

Val: This is America, Tom.

Tom: Workin' for?

Val: Justice.

Tom: Buyin' judges.

Val: People like wealth.

Tom: In a thief's pocket?

Val: Don't ask.

Tom: Gotta ask.

Val: We're done.

Tom: Think?

Val: One chance.

Tom: Yeah?

Val: Employees.

Tom: What?

Val: Say instructions from the top.

Tom: From him.
Val: The pinnacle.
Tom: We need?
Val: Many as we can.
Tom: I'm on it.
He turns to leave.
Val: Tom?
He stops.
Val: Careful.
Tom: Sure.

BLACKOUT

SCENE THIRTEEN

Pipeline. George and Tom.

George: Not my job.
Tom: Never?
George: Once in a way.
Tom: Trained?
George: Uh-uh.
Tom: Instructions from the top?
George: The top?
Tom: Man himself.
George: No.
Tom: Take this, say that.
George: No.
Tom: Honest man?
George: Sure.
Tom: Proud?
George: Sure.
Tom: Worked all your life?
George: Yeah.
Tom: Honest buck?
George: That's it.
Tom: American way?
George: Yes, sir.
Tom: You and me steal some oil?
George: Cop.
Tom: Cop's don't steal?
George: Most.
Tom: Secret.
George: No.
Tom: Company says steal, you steal?
George: No.
Tom (inspecting pipe): Fix this?

George: My job.
Tom: Rust.
George: Some.
Tom: Looks bad.
George: Touch that !
Tom: Hey.
George: Company property.
Tom: Blow?
George: No
Tom: Looks bad.
George: Last months.
Tom: Don't say?
George: Sure.
Tom: Fix it, gotta shut it down?
George: Sure.
Tom: How long?
George: Month.
Tom: Lotta oil.
George: Sure.
Tom: That blows, lotta oil.
George: Won't.
Tom: Sent a report?
George: Yeah.
Tom: See it?
George: No copy.
Tom: No kiddin'.
George: True.
Tom: One copy.
George: Sure.
Tom: Remember it?
George: Kinda.
Tom: Need fixin'?
George: Little while.
Tom: Rust last a little while?

George: Sure.
Tom: Responsibility.
George: My job.
Tom: Someone's life.
George: Company see to it.
Tom: Company honest?
George: Enough.
Tom: Gotta make money.
George: Business.
Tom: Pipe like that blows.
George: Won't.
Tom: Kids play here?
George; Kids?
Tom: Yeah. Town nearby.
George: Nah.
Tom: Kids like it. Desert. Pipeline.
George: Company land.
Tom: Kids know the law?
George: No kids.
Tom: Know William Farmer?
George: No.
Tom: Chief.
George: Police?
Tom: Native Americans.
George: Don't know' em.
Tom: Said company stole their oil.

George: Proof?
Tom: Changed his mind.
George: Lying.
Tom: Persuaded.
George: Who knows?
Tom: Someone.
George: Not me.

Tom: Take this, say that.

George: Not me.

Tom: Ten million a year.

George (shaking head): My business.

Tom: Whose business?

George: Company.

Tom: Company got a conscience?

George: I guess.

Tom: Company a person?

George: A person?

Tom: Yeah.

George: Company's a company.

Tom: Whose responsible?

George: Beats me.

Tom: We are.

George: Do my job.

Tom: Me too.

George: Sure.

Tom: Crooks behind bars.

George: Sure.

Tom: Ten million a year.

George: He says.

Tom: Hear anything?

George: Nope.

Tom: Maybe in a bar.

George: Nope.

Tom: Guy says took this, said that.

George: Nope.

Tom: Never?

George: Never.

Tom: America.

George: Sure.

Tom: Law for the little guy.

George: Great country.

Tom: We're the little guys, George.
George: Sure.
Tom: Your boss is a crook.
George: You say.

BLACKOUT

SCENE FOURTEEN

Tom at home on sofa, beer in hand. Mobile rings.

Tom: Hello, Sam.
Sam: Got a minute?
Tom: Ten p.m.
Sam: I know.
Tom: Agents gotta sleep.
Sam: Somethin' for ya.
Tom: Murder?
Sam: Better.
Tom: Drugs?
Sam: Better.
Tom: Mob?
Sam: Opportunity.
Tom: My age?
Sam: Miami.
Tom: Holiday?
Sam: Transfer?
Tom: Miami.
Sam: Home.
Tom: How come?
Sam: Vacancy.
Tom: My name on it.
Sam: Why not?
Tom: I got cases.
Sam: Agents got cases.
Tom: You know.
Sam: What?
Tom: Big guys.
Sam: Miami, Tom.
Tom: Now?
Sam: Yeah.

Tom: Outta nowhere.

Sam: Way it works.

Tom: I know.

Sam: Say no, it's gone.

Tom: It is?

Sam: People like Miami.

Tom: Say no now?

Sam: Twenty-four hours.

Tom: A week.

Sam: Too long.

Tom: I'm stayin'.

Sam: You are?

Tom: Sure.

Sam: Home, Tom.

Tom: I visit.

Sam: Key West.

Tom: Crime.

Sam: Dry Tortugas.

Tom: Racism.

Sam: Family?

Tom: Sure.

Sam: Opportunity, Tom.

Tom: Be more.

Sam: Don't count on it.

Tom: No?

Sam: No.

Tom: Got cases.

Sam: Same old.

Tom: My life.

Sam: City life.

Tom: I'm okay.

Sam: Sure.

Tom: Outta nowhere.

Sam: Way it is.

Tom: On to somethin'.

Sam: I know.

Tom: Big guys going to jail.

Sam: Big guys, little guys.

Tom: Ten million a year.

Sam: Small potatoes.

Tom: I got 'em.

Sam: You think?

Tom: I know.

Sam: Retire here?

Tom: Retire?

Sam: Sure.

Tom: Got years.

Sam: Gotta plan.

Tom: I plan.

Sam: House paid?

Tom: What?

Sam: Nice place in Miami.

Tom: Doin' okay.

Sam: What's okay?

Tom: We get by.

Sam: Yours.

Tom: What?

Sam: Five bedrooms.

Tom: I need five?

Sam: Miami. People like to visit.

Tom: Whose house?

Sam: Ours.

Tom: The Police Department?

Sam: Friends.

Tom: Crooks?

Sam: All legal.

Tom: Want me off the case, Sam?

Sam: Opportunity, Tom.

Tom: Got one.

Sam: Heard the guagers aren't singing.

Tom: Who cares?

Sam: This fails, you're finished.

Tom: You think?

Sam: Step back.

Tom: I like work.

Sam: Ease off the gas.

Tom: Not old.

Sam: Documents destroyed.

Tom: They say.

Sam: Wild goose chase.

Tom: Got copies.

Sam: You have?

Tom: Will.

Sam: You don't, too bad.

Tom: I'm stayin'.

Sam: Little lady ?

Tom: Happy.

Sam: Like Florida?

Tom: Scared of alligators.

Sam: Not all in Miami, Tom.

Tom: Don't say.

Sam: Twenty-four hours.

Tom: Getting' soft.

Sam: Not a minute more.

Tom: Don't need it.

BLACKOUT

SCENE FIFTEEN

Office. Val and Tom.

Val: Miami?
Tom: Home.
Val: Yeah?
Tom: Born.
Val: Outta nowhere.
Tom: Way it is.
Val (shakes head): Wow.
Tom: Got 'em.
Val: You think?
Tom: Sure.
Val: No documents.
Tom: Employees.
Val: Zipped.
Tom: Be okay.
Val: Easy life.
Tom: Easier.
Val: Bucks?
Tom: Nope.
Val: Home.
Tom: Sure.
Val: Ten million a year.
Tom: Evidence is somewhere.
Val: William Framer says no.
Tom: Leaned on.
Val: Got the weight.
Tom: Don't give up.
Val: Lean on everyone.
Tom: Got the power.
Val: Sure.
Tom: America.

Val: Sure.

Tom: Law's for the little guy.

Val: On my own.

Tom: On your own. Grand Jury.

Val: Want 'em behind bars?

Tom: Justice.

Val: You and me.

Tom: Who am I?

Val: They buy us.

Tom: Not me.

Val: No?

Tom: No.

Val: Judges.

Tom: Law's the law.

Val: Judges decide.

Tom: Can't buy the system.

Val: Know how many?

Tom: No.

Val: Thousand.

Tom: Yeah?

Val: Hayek.

Tom: They swallow that?

Val: America.

Tom: Someone'll squeal.

Val: Soon?

Tom: Law's slow.

Val: They're fast.

Tom: Guy in a bar.

Val: Buying senators.

Tom: Some.

Val: Big government.

Tom: Big government this, big government that. Crooks.

Val: With money.

Tom: Crooks.

Val: In suits.

Tom: Folks don't like crooks.

Val: Little crooks.

Tom: Any.

Val: Kid steals your car radio he's a crook. Company steals ten million dollars of oil it's business.

Tom: Not politics. Law.

Val: Sure.

Tom: I'm for business.

Val: Me too.

Tom: Honest.

Val: What's honest?

Tom: Legal.

Val: Buy a good lawyer.

Tom: No law, what happens?

Val: Wild west?

Tom: No business.

Val: Crooked business.

Tom: Mafia.

Val: Make money.

Tom: Kill the competition.

Val: Business not do that?

Tom: Country's gotta be clean.

Val: Miami?

Tom: Sure. Work to do.

Val: Seen the stats?

Tom: Yeah.

Val: Do?

Tom: Lock 'em up.

Val: Big university for crime.

Tom: What else?

Val: What are we?

Tom: Do our jobs.

Val: Sure. Miami, Tom.

Tom: Opportunity, Val.
Val: I know.
Tom: Lock 'em up, Val.
Val: You stay we will.
Tom: Val.
Val: Take your place?
Tom: Who knows?
Val: I get offered Miami.
They laugh.
Tom: Home?
Val: New York.
Tom: Lock 'em up.
Val: Good luck, Tom.

BLACKOUT

SCENE SIXTEEN

As scene one. Howard and Rich on sofa. Howard on mobile.

Howard: Senator?
Fred: Howard? Well ?
Howard: Fine.
Fred: Do for ya ?
Howard: Oil business. Rich here with me.
Fred: Evidence?
Howard: You're right. This attorney.
Fred: Yeah?
Howard: Val Payne.
Fred: Trouble?
Howard: Crusade.
Fred: Yeah?
Howard: FBI guy.
Fred: Gone?
Howard: Miami.
Fred: Alligator dinner.
They laugh.
Howard: We were thinkin'.
Fred: Yeah?
Howard: Phil Read ambitious?
Fred: Sure.
Howard nods to Rich.
Howard: Might run for something?
Fred: Might.
Howard: Find him somethin'?
Fred: Maybe.
Howard: He leaves, you choose.
Fred: I do.
Howard: Rich was thinkin'.
Fred: Yeah?

Howard: Jim Close.

Fred: Good guy.

Howard: Rich says.

Fred: Diamond.

Howard: Knows his Hayek?

Fred: Sure.

Howard: Thing is.

Fred: Yeah?

Howard: Speed.

Fred: Right.

Howard: This attorney.

Fred: Nuisance.

Howard: You bet. Frustrated.

Fred: You think.

Howard: Needs a good you know what.

Fred: Do the job?

Howard: My dog.

They laugh.

Fred: Push Phil.

Howard: Soon?

Fred: Golf. Tomorrow. Weekend.

Howard: Fine. (Rich signals for phone. Howard passes it.)

Rich: Fred?

Fred: Good to hear ya, Rich?

Rich: Phil Read.

Fred: Yeah.

Rich: Know him well?

Fred: Pretty?

Rich: Liberal?

Fred: Sure.

Rich: Communist?

Fred: Say not.

Rich: Scratch a liberal, Fred.

Fred: Sure.

Rich: Attorney wants me in jail.

Fred: Crazy.

Rich: Government is anti-business.

Fred: Well, Bush…

Rich: Bush?

Fred: Our man.

Rich: Bush on board with the judges thing?

Fred: Maybe.

Rich: No room for maybe.

Fred: Right.

Rich: Maybe is the death of business.

Fred: I know.

Rich: Business needs?

Fred: Certainty.

Rich: Absolute.

Fred: Gotta have it.

Rich: Maybe this, maybe that. Next thing is communism.

Fred: True.

Rich: Way to certainty?

Fred: Control.

Rich: Power.

Fred: You bet.

Rich: Democracy will kill this country.

Fred: Irresponsible voters.

Rich: Millions.

Fred: Gotta control 'em.

Rich: Take away the vote.

Fred: Tricky.

Rich: They vote, we rule.

Fred: That's it.

Rich: That's fair.

Fred: Absolutely.

Rich: Who made this country?

Fred: Businessmen.

Rich: Told what to do by blacks from the projects?

Fred: Joke.

Rich: They have the vote?

Fred: I know.

Rich: Trailer trash.

Fred: Illiterates.

Rich: They rule me?

Fred: Crazy.

Rich: Democracy's gone crazy.

Fred: Outta line.

Rich: Meddlin'.

Fred: Dirty fingers.

Rich: Business gotta rule.

Fred: That's fair.

Rich: We made this country.

Fred: Founding fathers want blacks to rule?

Rich: So right. Blacks. Hispanics. Communists.

Fred; Danger.

Rich: This attorney.

Fred: Payne.

Rich: She is.

Fred: Needs a good looking after.

Rich: Me in jail.

Fred: Ain't happenin'.

Rich: Justice?

Fred: No, sir.

Rich: We build this country they want us in jail?

Fred: Gone crazy.

Rich: Bill Price ready?

Fred: Will be.

Rich: Gotta move fast.

Fred: I know.

Rich: Jim Close okay?

Fred: Good guy.

Rich: Payne gotta go.

Fred: Sure thing.

Rich: Jim Close get federal judge?

Fred: Federal judge?

Rich: You nominate.

Fred: Well…

Rich: Certainty, Fred.

Fred: Do what I can.

Rich: What you can?

Fred: President gotta confirm.

Rich: Know that.

Fred: Well…

Rich: President our man or ain't he?

Fred: Protocol…

Rich: Protocol this, protocol that. Next thing a communist in the White House.

Fred: Sure.

Rich: Or a black.

Fred: I know.

Rich: Too much democracy, Fred.

Fred: You're right.

Rich: People think for themselves what you get?

Fred: I know.

Rich: Democracy's gone too far.

Fred: Some.

Rich: Country needs a business insurrection.

Fred: Right.

Rich: You in?

Fred: I'm in.

Rich: Fast.

BLACKOUT

SCENE SEVENTEEN

Auto-shop. William Farmer and Joe Brady seated.

Joe: Forever.
William: Always.
Joe: Reservation?
William: Chief.
Joe: No kiddin'?
William (holds out hand): William Farmer.
Joe: Joe Brady. Pleased.
William: Station wagon hit a rock.
Joe: Yeah?
William: Crippled.
Joe: Tyres.
William: Lotta miles?
Joe: Some. Worked on your land.
William: Yeah?
Joe: Oil.
William: You did?
Joe: Years.
William: Like it?
Joe: Like workin?
William: Sure.
Joe (shaking his head): I could tell ya.
William: Yeah?
Joe: I saw.
William: What?
Joe: Shouldn't say.
William: Bad?
Joe: Real bad.
William: Safety?
Joe: That !
William: Folk hurt.

Joe: I could tell ya.

William: We believed.

Joe: Yeah?

William: Theft.

Joe: You did?

William: Company came. Auditor.

Joe: So?

William: We owed twenty-two thousand bucks.

Joe: Man.

William: Brains (he taps his forehead).

Joe: You think?

William: Harvard. Princeton.

Joe: Believe 'em.

William: Figures don't lie.

Joe (shaking his head) Oh boy.

William: Quadratics.

Joe: What?

William: Guy said. Differential. Denominator. Smart stuff.

Joe (shaking head): Smart.

William: Had no one.

Joe: Accountant?

William: No.

Joe: I could tell ya.

William: Yeah?

Joe: I saw.

William: What?

Joe: Your people.

William: My people.

Joe: Robbed.

William: You saw?

Joe: I did it.

William: You?

Joe: And the rest.

William: Why?

Joe: Gotta eat.

William: Gotta steal?

Joe: Get fired.

William: Fired for honesty?

Joe: World works, William.

William: Not ours.

Joe: Got robbed.

William: You did that?

Joe: Company tells ya.

William: Who?

Joe: Who?

William: Yeah.

Joe: I dunno. Top man.

William: Spoke to ya?

Joe: No.

William: Who?

Joe: Some guy.

William: Name?

Joe: One guy. Two guys.

William: Told ya?

Joe: Sure.

William: Steal or fired.

Joe: Sure. Kinda. Take this, say that.

William: How much?

Joe: Millions.

William: You?

Joe: Everyone.

William: How long?

Joe: Years.

William: Twenty?

Joe: Me? Seven. Eight.

William: That time.

Joe: Sure.

William: Our oil.

Joe: I got nothin'.

William: I know.

Joe: Sorry, man.

William: Your fault.

Joe: Get fired, my kids don't eat.

William: Sure.

Joe: Company says.

William: Yeah.

Joe: Do somethin'.

William: Too late.

Joe: Law asleep?

William: Badly informed.

Joe: Duped.

William: Yeah.

Joe: Gotta do somethin'.

William: Country built on robbing us.

Joe: Need a lawyer.

William: They buy 'em.

Joe: You?

William: We billionaires?

Joe: This is America.

William: Sure.

Joe: Law for the little guy.

William: Yeah.

BLACKOUT

SCENE EIGHTEEN

Office. Val Payne on mobile.

Val: Phil?
Phil: Val? Heard?
Val: Yeah.
Phil: Okay?
Val: Your life.
Phil: Opportunity.
Val: Sure.
Phil: Outta the blue.
Val: Yeah.
Phil: Fred Buxton.
Val: I know.
Phil: My back.
Val: He has.
Phil: Be fine.
Val: Yeah. He'll choose.
Phil: Who?
Val: Fred.
Phil: Successor?
Val; Yeah.
Phil: Sure.
Val: Idea?
Phil: No. Well, maybe Jim Close.
Val: You think?
Phil: Maybe. Okay with that?
Val: Good lawyer?
Phil: I guess.
Val: Political hack?
Phil: Well..
Val: Buxton's no liberal.
Phil: No, Val. You'll be okay.

Val: Sure. This oil thing.

Phil: Keep going.

Val: Want him behind bars.

Phil: Get the proof.

Val: Someone spoken to Buxton?

Phil: You think.

Val: I heard.

Phil: Who?

Val: P.R. man.

Phil: Simon?

Val: Yeah.

Phil: Maybe.

Val: Talking 'bout the weather?

Phil: I know, Val.

Val: Judges gettin' bought.

Phil: Law's the law.

Val: You know.

Phil: Evidence speaks.

Val: Gets a chance.

Phil: How not?

Val: Dunno.

Phil: Keep on.

Val: Sure. Some judge says drop it.

Phil: Maybe.

Val: Big guys go free.

Phil: Shit happens.

Val: Ten million a year, Phil.

Phil: Done what you can.

Val: Enough?

Phil: Sure.

Val: Justice?

Phil: Blind.

Val: Sees dollars.

Phil: Done what you can, Val.

Val: Shit happens.

BLACKOUT

SCENE NINETEEN

Office. Val on mobile.

Tom: Val?
Val: Hi,Tom.
Tom: You quit?
Val: Had to.
Tom: Yeah?
Val: Jim Close.
Tom: Bully?
Val: Hack.
Tom: Sure.
Val: Like you.
Tom: Opportunity?
Val: Yeah. Get out.
Tom: New job?
Val: No.
Tom: Val, you should.
Val: I should?
Tom: You're good.
Val: You too.
Tom: I'm working.
Val: Oil?
Tom: Drugs.
Val: Pays well.
Tom: Gotta do it.
Val: Sure.
Tom: Gangsters.
Val: Right.
Tom: Psychopaths.
Val: True.
Tom: Clean up the streets.
Val: Big guys.

Tom: Some.

Val: Little guys do the dirt.

Tom: Sure.

Val: Stayed here, we'd've had him.

Tom: I know.

Val: On my own.

Tom: Close against you?

Val: Buxton's man.

Tom: Buxton interfere?

Val: No.

Tom: Close say back off?

Val: Look after business.

Tom: America, Val.

Val: Drugs a business, Tom?

Tom: Economy needs oil.

Val: Society needs opiods.

Tom: Oil men shoot out on the street?

Val: Cleverer.

Tom: Coulda had him.

Val: Shoulda stayed, Tom.

Tom: You?

Val: I'm a lawyer.

Tom: Good one.

Val: Office full of politics.

Tom: Tell him?

Val: My boss.

Tom: Your rights.

Val: Things we can't see, Tom.

Tom: Yeah?

Val: Buying his way out.

Tom: If I'd stayed..

Val: If.

Tom: Those documents.

Val: Yeah.

Tom: New guy find copies?

Val: You know.

Tom: Push him?

Val: Close not interested.

Tom: Do it.

Val: Too late, Tom.

Tom: If I'd stayed…

Val: Opportunity.

Tom: Yeah.

Val: Outta the blue.

Tom: Yeah.

Val: They beat us, Tom.

Tom: Maybe.

Val: They beat the law.

BLACKOUT

SCENE TWENTY

As scene one. Rich and Ken on sofa.

Ken: Done.
Rich: Nominated?
Ken: Uh-uh.
Rich: Buxton's our guy.
Ken; Good guy.
Rich: President like Close?
Ken: President know?
Rich: Gotta confirm?
Ken: Sure.
Rich: Finds out.
Ken: Gets told.
Rich: Turn him down?
Ken: Can.
Rich: You think?
Ken: Objection?
Rich: Democrats. Corruption this, corruption that.
Ken: President gonna listen?
Rich: Turns him down, maybe I go to prison.
Ken: Won't happen.
Rich: How long?
Ken: Few months.
Rich: Months?
Ken: Yeah.
Rich: Too long.
Ken: Law is slow.
Rich: Speed it up.
Ken: Rouse suspicion.
Rich: FBI find one document, I'm locked up.
Ken: FBI guy's gone.
Rich: Who's on it?

Ken: Guy knows nothin'.

Rich: Keen?

Ken: No background.

Rich: Attorney speak to him?

Ken: Gone.

Rich: One document.

Ken: I know.

Rich: One canary.

Ken: We're safe.

Rich: Close confirmed, he'll drop?

Ken: Well..

Rich: Well?

Ken: Honest guy.

Rich: I'm honest.

Ken: Sure.

Rich: Business is tough.

Ken: Right.

Rich: Rules gotta bend.

Ken: They do.

Rich: Honest this, honest that. Next thing, communism.

Ken: Correct.

Rich: Stole a bit o' oil.

Ken: Trivial.

Rich: Indians know what to do ?

Ken: No idea.

Rich: Leave that stuff in the ground.

Ken; Crazy.

Rich: That's billions.

Ken: Lost.

Rich: Forever.

Ken: Irresponsible.

Rich: Primitive.

Ken: Correct.

Rich: Who built business?

Ken: Entrepreneurs.
Rich: Indians?
Ken: Tcha.
Rich: Extraction is free?
Ken: Expensive.
Rich: Who pays?
Ken: You.
Rich: I filch. Take this, say that. Business.
Ken: It is.
Rich: Selling your car you tell the truth?
Ken: No one.
Rich: Kindergarten?
Ken: Big boys.
Rich: Survive in business?
Ken: Dodge and weave.
Rich: Close gotta drop.
Ken: Slowly.
Rich: Slowly I'm in prison.
Ken: Relax. Got nothin'.
Rich: One document.
Ken: Gone.
Rich: One canary.
Ken: We're safe.

BLACKOUT

SCENE TWENTY ONE

Office. Ken and Jim Close, fifty.

Ken: Right thing.
Close: Maybe.
Ken: Maybe?
Close: Law's the law.
Ken: Sure. Grateful.
Close (shaking head): My decision.
Ken: No?
Close: Assistant attorney.
Ken: No kiddin'?
Close: Know 100omething'?
Ken: Me?
Close: Yeah.
Ken: Nope.
Close: Senators wrote me.
Ken: I heard.
Close: Complained to the FBI.
Ken: Those guys.
Close: Those guys?
Ken: You know.
Close: I do?
Ken: Snooping here, snooping there.
Close: Crime is crime.
Ken: Sure.
Close: Stealin' oil.
Ken: From Indians?
Close: Anyone.
Ken: Well..
Close: Well ?
Ken: Big man's pleased.
Close: Off the hook.

Ken: Never on.
Close: I heard.
Ken: Yeah?
Close: Guy in an autoshop.
Ken: What's that?
Close: Told William Farmer.
Ken: Trust him?
Close: Trained to mismeasure.
Ken: Some guy.
Close: Worked for your big man.
Ken: He says.
Close: Case can re-open.
Ken: Evidence.
Close: Guy says.
Ken: Liar.
Close: For ?
Ken: Little guy wants to be big guy.
Close: Val Payne was sure.
Ken: She quit.
Close: Me.
Ken: Chased her out.
Close: "Political hack".
Ken: Good.
Close: Didn't like her.
Ken: Who does?
Close: Liberal.
Ken: Communist.
Close: Good lawyer.
Ken: Yeah.
Close: Tenacious.
Ken: Pig-headed.
Close: Tom Ralston stayed. Your man behind bars.
Ken: You think?
Close: She said.

Ken: She quit.

Close: Yeah.

Ken: Good job.

Close: What?

Ken: Forced her out.

Close: Not for your man.

Ken: No?

Close: Open mind.

Ken: Dropped the case.

Close: Had to.

Ken: Assistant attorney was right.

Close: Maybe.

Ken: Good man.

Close: Good lawyer.

Ken: Right.

Close: Nobody buys me.

Ken: Bought him?

Close: Who knows?

Ken: Who?

Close: What I heard?

Ken: Brother going for civil suit.

Close: You don't say?

Ken: Know him?

Ken: Nope.

Close: Found Tom Ralston.

Ken: Yeah.

Close: Not over.

Ken: Evidence?

Close: One document.

Ken: Gone.

Close: One canary.

Ken: We're safe.

Close: You think?

BLACKOUT

SCENE TWENTY-TWO

An office. Rich and Ken.

Rich: Jobs.
Ken: How many?
Rich: Half a million. More.
Ken: Say.
Rich: Half a million, easy.
Ken: Key states.
Rich: Yeah.
Ken: Wyoming, Texas, North Dakota, Louisiana, West Virginia.
Rich: Pressure.
Ken: American Energy Alliance.
Rich: Message?
Ken: Costs up, competitiveness down, jobs gone.
Rich: One group?
Ken: Citizens for a Sound Economy.
Rich: Senators?
Ken: Enough.
Rich: People get hold of it, that's trouble.
Ken: People won't know.
Rich: Heard the green stuff?
Ken: Some.
Rich: Jobs in new industries.
Ken: Keep it quiet.
Rich: Swamp the media.
Ken: On our side.
Rich: Gore is hugging trees.
Ken: It's a tax.
Rich: Point of production.
Ken: Sure.
Rich: People don't notice.

Ken: Make 'em notice.

Rich: Sierra Club.

ken: Who's heard of 'em?

Rich: National Resources Defence Council.

Ken: They got money?

Rich: Heard the CEOs?

Ken: What's wrong with those guys?

Rich: Cuts pollution.

Ken: Adam Smith worry about pollution?

Rich: Good for work and investment.

Ken: Bamboozled.

Rich: By?

Ken: Clinton.

Rich: Gore's pushing.

Ken: Cornbelt senators.

Rich: Yeah?

Ken: Ethanol.

Rich: They're opposed?

Ken: Ethanol exempt.

Rich: Only?

Ken: Beginning.

Rich: You think?

Ken: Clinton's weak.

Rich: We got him?

Ken: Exempts ethanol, the thing collapses.

Rich: He will?

Ken: Pressure.

Rich: Who?

Ken: Affordable Energy Alliance.

Rich: That all?

Ken: American Petroleum Institute.

Rich: Little people.

Ken: Farmers.

Rich: Good.

Ken: Diesel fuel.

Rich: Tractors.

Ken: Harvesters.

Rich: Feed the people.

Ken: Right.

Rich: Grazing fees.

Ken: Don't like 'em.

Rich: Gotta reduce the deficit.

Ken: Sure.

Rich: Popular.

Ken: It is.

Rich: Raise the money somehow.

Ken: Cut welfare.

Rich: Clinton?

Ken: He's weak.

Rich: His base.

Ken: Middle classes.

Rich: BTU protects 'em.

Ken: Sure. And the poor.

Rich: Five hundred billion dollars.

Ken: Cut the programs.

Rich: Gore?

Ken: Key senators.

Rich: Who?

Ken: Finance committee.

Rich: Eleven to nine.

Ken: Exactly.

Rich: People gotta back 'em.

Ken: Ads.

Rich: Papers?

Ken: Yeah. TV. Louisiana, Oklahoma, Montana, North Dakota.

Rich: Mailings?

Ken: Sure. Utilities.

Rich: They will?

Ken: Their profits.

Rich: Hydro-power.

Ken: Right.

Rich: Aluminium?

Ken: Need electricity.

Rich: Clean water.

Ken: I know.

Rich: People'll like that.

Ken: If they know.

Rich: They won't ?

Ken: Never.

Rich: Environmentalists everywhere.

Ken: No money.

Rich: Get big, we're done.

Ken: Country's done.

Rich: Poor got to lose?

Ken: Irresponsible.

Rich: They vote, I pay.

Ken: They care?

Rich: Vote with their welfare cheque.

Ken: Cut it.

Rich: Five hundred billion.

Ken: Sure.

Rich: Gotta raise some.

Ken: Tax gasoline.

Rich: Hit the middle classes.

Ken: So?

Rich: They go left.

Ken: They won't.

Rich: The poor?

Ken: They know?

Rich: Get 'em on our side.

Ken: Patriotism.

Rich: America first.
Ken: They like it.
Rich: Who's the enemy?
Ken: Muslims. Arabs.
Rich: China.
Ken: Sure.
Rich: Give 'em the flag and cut their welfare.
Ken: That's it.
Rich: Tree huggers American?
Ken: Gotta destroy to build.
Rich: Redskins build anything?
Ken: Wigwams.
Rich: Nader build anything?
Ken: Failure.
Rich: That guy American?
Ken: Communist.
Rich: Anything wrong with the Corsair?
Ken: Great car.
Rich: How many sold?
Ken: Millions.
Rich: Business gives people a car, Nader snipes.
Ken: That's communism.
Rich: Was Powell right?
Ken: You kiddin' me?
Rich: Where's the negativity?
Ken: Everywhere.
Rich: Church on our side?
Ken: Some.
Rich: Pulpit says government this, social justice that.
Ken: Purge 'em.
Rich: Liberals doin' in the church?
Ken: Don't immanentize the eschaton.
They laugh.
Rich: What's heaven for?

Ken: The afterlife is the real life.

Rich: Heaven on earth?

Ken: Sick idea.

Rich: Take tobacco.

Ken: Great business.

Rich: Cancer this, heart disease that.

Ken: Give people choice.

Rich: Phillip Morris American?

Ken: Pure.

Rich: Newspapers, intellectuals, cancer this, heart disease that.

Ken: Keep an eye on 'em.

Rich: Sigma Society. Right idea.

Ken: You bet.

Rich: Earhart foundation.

Ken: People like charity.

Rich: That's it.

Ken: Scaife.

Rich: That's right.

Ken: Smith Richardson.

Rich: Intellectuals on our side.

Ken: Journals, think-tanks, professorships..

Rich: Keep the left out.

Ken: Pay for free thinking.

Rich: People like that.

Ken: They do.

Rich: Carthage Foundation.

Ken: Positive voices.

Rich: Nader, what's he saying?

Ken: Consumerism is communism.

Rich: Does business know?

Ken: Business gives the people what they want.

Rich: Who criticises?

Ken: Enemies of the people.

Rich: Of democracy.

Ken: Right.

Rich: American Enterprise Institute.

Ken: Doin' the work.

Rich: New Deal?

Ken: Bad time.

Rich: That American?

Ken: Anti-American.

Rich: Public this, public that.

Ken: Where's enterprise?

Rich: Where's liberty?

Ken: Let people choose.

Rich: People choose socialism?

Ken: They gotta be stopped.

Rich: Secretly.

Ken: Sure.

Rich: People hear, BTU tax, saves the planet. What happens?

Ken: Save the planet, destroy business.

Rich: Back to wigwams.

Ken: Hunting bison.

Rich: Progress?

Ken: Keep it quiet.

Rich: Sierra Club?

Ken: Hikers.

Rich: Back to nature.

Ken: What's nature?

Rich: Business.

Ken: You got it.

Rich: Redskins find oil?

Ken: Sat on it.

Rich: Thousandsa years.

Ken: Stasis.

Rich: Did we steal?

Ken: Did they have it?

Rich: Underground.

Ken: Could they get it?
Rich: Their land, so what?
Ken: So what?
Rich: We learned.
Ken: We did.
Rich: Business gotta beat government.
Ken: Else?
Rich: Communism.
Ken: Serfdom.
Rich: The man says.

BLACKOUT

SCENE TWENTY-THREE

As scene one. Rich and Bev on sofa. Rich on mobile. Bev reading women's magazine. Every few seconds she shoves it under Rich's nose. He nods. Smiles.

Rich: Ken?
Ken: Bad news.
Rich: How bad?
Ken: Ninety thousand gallons.
Rich: Contained.
Ken: No.
Rich: The law?
Ken: Fine.
Rich: Prison.
Ken. Not you.
Rich: Who?
Ken: Who's responsible?
Rich: Employees.
Ken: Correct.
Rich: Incompetent.
Ken: Got it.
Rich: Dishonest.
Ken: To the bone.
Rich: Injured.
Ken: No one.
Rich: Buxton?
Ken: Speaking to the President.
Rich: How much?
Ken: I dunno. Twenty, thirty million.
Rich: Offer it.
Ken: Sure.
Rich: Outta court.
Ken: Best.

Rich: Media?

Ken: On it.

Rich: Shut those guys up.

Ken: First amendment.

Rich: First amendment this, first amendment that. Next thing, communism.

Ken: Play it down.

Rich: How?

Ken: Bad employees.

Rich: Right.

Ken: Didn't report.

Rich: Proof?

Ken: Fabricate.

Rich: Careful.

Ken: Got experts.

Rich: President with us?

Ken: Will be.

Rich: Tree huggers on the march.

Ken: Who cares?

Rich: Environment this, environment that. Business first.

Ken: People know.

Rich: America first.

Ken: Always.

Rich: Save the planet. What for?

Ken: Right.

Rich: For communism?

Ken: No, sir.

Rich: Business goes down, take the planet with us.

Ken: Absolutely.

Rich: Ninety thousand?

Ken: Yup.

Rich: Lotta oil.

Ken: Some.

Rich: Say forty thousand.

Ken: Maybe. Fifty.

Rich: Gonna know?

Ken: Get your truth in first.

Rich: Few journalists need the money.

Ken: They'll bite.

Rich: Sure no prison?

Ken: No chance.

BLACKOUT

SCENE TWENTY-FOUR

Unincorporated community. Texas. Caroline, 17, standing alone.

Caroline: Pop.
Pop (off throughout scene) : Yeah?
Caroline: Gas.
Pop: Again.
Caroline (sniffs the air): I get it.
Pop: Wait a while.
Caroline: Strong.
Pop: Come inside.
Caroline: Better go tell.
Pop: No. Come inside.
Caroline: Could be dangerous, pop.
Pop: Yeah. Come inside.
Caroline: I dunno.
Pop: Give it a while.
Caroline: You think?
Pop: Small leak.
Caroline (sniffs the air again): Ain't small.
Pop: Don't breathe that stuff.
Caroline: Gotta breathe.
Pop: Come inside.
Caroline: Take the station wagon?
Pop: No, Caroline. Come inside here.
Caroline: Gotta tell someone, pop.
Pop: Think no one is?
Caroline: Phoned?
Pop: Not yet.
Caroline: Gonna?
Pop: Yeah.
Caroline: Who?

Pop: Sheriff.

Caroline: Do anythin'?

Pop: Responsibility.

Caroline: Last time?

Pop: Last time was okay.

Caroline: Worse.

Pop: Yeah?

Caroline (sniffs): Sure.

Pop: You come in here.

Caroline: There in ten minutes.

Pop: Give it time.

Caroline: Might get worse.

Pop: Might get better.

Caroline: John come with me.

Pop: He there?

Caroline: No. Come if I yell.

Pop: Leave him be.

Caroline: Reckon that pipe's done for.

Pop: Leaks all the time.

Caroline: Like this.

Pop: Let it be. Come inside.

Caroline: Smell it?

Pop: No.

Caroline: Open the door.

Pop: No.

Caroline: John come with me I'll be safe.

Pop: Leave the boy be, Caroline.

Caroline: I dunno.

Pop: Folks'll be phonin' right now.

Caroline: You?

Pop: Minute.

Caroline: We go they gotta listen.

Pop: Why?

Caroline: I smelt it.

Pop: Lots o' folks smelt it.

Caroline (shakes head): Like this.

Pop: Made some coffee.

Caroline: Okay.

Pop: Come in now.

Caroline: I dunno, pop.

Pop: Pie?

Caroline: Back in twenty.

Pop: Coffee's here.

Caroline: Keep it warm.

Pop: John there?

Caroline: No. (Calls). John ! Hey, John.!

John (off): Yeah?

Caroline: Gas. Takin' the station wagon. Comin'?

John: Where?

Caroline: Sheriff.

John: Okay.

Caroline: See ya, pop.

Pop: John goin?

Caroline: Yeah.

Pop: Take care now.

Caroline: John ! Station wagon.

She exits. Laughter off. Sound of station wagon doors closing. Engine starts and there is huge explosion which fills the auditorium with garish light and terrifying noise.

BLACKOUT

SCENE TWENTY-FIVE

As scene one. Rich on sofa, Ken pacing.

Ken: So two kids get scorched. Shit happens.
Rich: Prison?
Ken: Pay 'em off.
Rich: Court.
Ken: Maybe
Rich: How much.
Ken; Millions.
Rich: How many?
Ken: Maybe fifty.
Rich: I'm off the hook?
Ken: Sure.
Rich: Give him fifty.
Ken; You know these people.
Rich: What?
Ken: His daughter gets roasted. He wants his day. The newspapers. Have his say.
Rich: Let him.
Ken: Sure.
Rich: Fifty and say the right things. Tragic loss. Send flowers.
Ken: Sure. Maybe a hundred.
Rich: A hundred.
Ken: Depends.
Rich: On the judge?
Ken: Yeah.
Rich: Kids.
Ken: Sure.
Rich: Our fault?
Ken: Who cares?
Rich: They messed with the pipe?
Ken: They did?

Rich: Did they?

Ken: They didn't.

Rich: Maybe they did.

Ken; They did?

Rich: If they did.

Ken: If?

Rich: Not our fault.

Ken: Fault shmalt.

Rich: Media all over it.

Ken: Buy 'em.

Rich: Sure. But reputation.

Ken: Buy it.

Rich: Sure. A hundred?

Ken: Maybe. Maybe one fifty.

Rich: One fifty?

Ken: Young kids.

Rich: Outta court?

Ken: Offer.

Rich: Give him a hundred. The other kid?

Ken: Fifty.

Rich: You think?

Ken: Sure.

Rich: One fifty and they shut their mouths.

Ken: They do.

Rich No interviews.

Ken: Got it.

Rich: Gonna know?

Ken: Liberals, tree-huggers. Who listens?

Rich: Shut 'em up.

Ken: Let 'em gabble.

Rich: Company gotta look good.

Ken: Makes money?

Rich: Gotta look good when I'm gone.

Ken: We're gone, who cares?

Rich: Got the money, Ken. Place in history.

Ken: Assured.

Rich: People gonna write about this?

Ken: Let 'em write.

Rich: Faulty pipe this, faulty pipe that. What happens to business?

Ken: Liberals.

Rich: Communists.

Ken: Who listens?

Rich: Gotta shut those people up.

Ken: Sure.

Rich: That's freedom.

Ken: Free speech.

Rich: That's it.

Ken: Free speech is business speech.

Rich: Right.

Ken: No one listens.

Rich: I pay, I want silence.

Ken: Correct.

Rich: Tragic accident.

Ken: It was.

Rich: Company innocent.

Ken: Always.

Rich: Deep regret. Loss of young life. That stuff.

Ken: Got it.

Rich: One fifty.

Ken: Yeah. Maybe two hundred.

Rich: Two hundred?

Ken: Maybe.

Rich: Pay it, but silence.

Ken: Absolutely.

BLACKOUT

SCENE TWENTY-SIX

Pipeline. George and Trig.

Trig: You hear?

George: What?

Trig: Caroline Sweeney.

George: Bad accident.

Trig: Methane.

George: Shouldn't started the truck.

Trig: Her fault, George!

George: No one's fault.

Trig: That pipe.

George: Still good.

Trig: Shoulda said.

George: No one round these parts.

Trig: Paper says she smelled it often.

George: Paper says.

Trig: Someone check that pipe?

George: Sure.

Trig: Like us.

George: I guess.

Trig: Put in a report.

George: Their job.

Trig: Like us.

George: Yep.

Trig: Supposin'.

George: Stop supposin'.

Trig: Supposin' that was us.

George: Not us.

Trig: Supposin'.

George: Drive yourself nuts supposin'.

Trig: You gotta think, George.

George: Ain't paid to think.

Trig: Company buy your mind?

George: Want your bonus, boy?

Trig: I gotta think.

George: Why?

Trig: We all gotta.

George: I don't.

Trig: You're thinkin'.

George: I am?

Trig; You're thinkin' company'll fire ya.

George: Do my job.

Trig: That's your thinkin', George.

George: Don't think about what ain't my business.

Trig: That blows it's our business.

George: Company's business.

Trig: Supposin' that was us.

George: Enough supposin'.

Trig: That pipe.

George: Not us.

Trig: Leakin' methane.

George: Leakin' pipe might last a long time.

Trig: We send a report.

George: Not us.

Trig: Tick those boxes.

George: Not me.

Trig: She starts the station wagon.

George: Bad accident.

Trig: Fireball.

George: Tragic accident.

Trig: Who's to blame?

George: Shit happens.

Trig: We are, George.

George: We ain't been near the place.

Trig: We're all responsible, George.

George: For what?

Trig: Everythin'.
George: Goin' nuts.
Trig: You gotta think.
George: Stop thinkin'.
Trig: That report.
George: Did our job.
Trig: Your kid, you say that?
George: Not my kid.
Trig: What goes around, George.
George: Drive yourself nuts.
Trig: Gonna tell somebody.
George: Who?
Trig: Dunno.
George: Keep you mouth shut, boy.
Trig: I gotta think.
George: Keep your thoughts to yourself.
Trig: Gotta tell someone, George.
George: Kid on the way.
Trig: Sure.
George: Need the money?
Trig: Sure.
George: Stick with the company.
Trig: Company murdered that girl.
George: Accident. Tragic loss of life.
Trig: That stuff.
George: Keep your mouth shut, Trig.

BLACKOUT

122

SCENE TWENTY-SEVEN

As scene one.

Ted: You're crooks.
Rich: We paid.
Ted: Twenty-five thousand documents falsified.
Rich: We paid.
Ted: Ten million a year.
Rich: All above board.
Ted: Jim Close dropped the case.
Rich: His decision.
Ted: You paid.
Rich: Never went near him.
Ted: Money has a long reach.
Rich: Close complained to the FBI.
Ted: So what?
Rich: Nobody nobbled him.
Ted: Not what Tom Ralston thinks.
Rich: Think what he likes.
Ted: Four years, ten million a year.
Rich: We paid.
Ted: Without me you'd've got away with it.
Rich: We did.
Ted: I told you I'd sue.
Rich: Throw your money away.
Ted: You pay, I pay.
Rich: Get what?
Ted: Justice.
Rich: Who's paying attention?
Ted: The world.
Rich: The world knows nothing.
Ted: You lost.
Rich; We settled.
Ted: Settling means guilt.

Rich: Our choice.

Ted: Those little guys.

Rich: Gave 'em jobs.

Ted: Made 'em liars.

Rich: Fed their kids.

Ted: Eric Denny.

Rich: Paid him well.

Ted: Said your business model based on theft.

Rich: Everybody steals.

Ted: They do?

Rich: Or lives in wigwams.

Ted: Give me the wigwam.

Rich: No bison left, Ted.

Ted: Just rattlesnakes.

Rich: Rattlesnakes prosper.

Ted: Johnny Hunter.

Rich: Thirty years work.

Ted: Mouth shut to keep his job.

Rich: Paid for his house.

Ted: Why'd he testify?

Rich: Pay him?

Ted; Tcha. Guy has a conscience.

Rich: Conscience didn't make America.

Ted: You aren't America, Rich.

Rich: America is business.

Ted: Honest business.

Rich: Ten million a year. Peanuts.

Ted: Amount makes no difference.

Rich: Never steal a spoon from a diner?

Ted: Stole their lives right there, Rich.

Rich: Indians? Sit on millions and do nothin'.

Ted: Their choice.

Rich: Give those people choice and where's progress?

Ted: Give you the choice and where's justice?

Rich: You're wealthy thanks to me.

Ted: Oh, I am so grateful.

Rich: No money no civil suit.

Ted: Money and honesty can live together.

Rich: My money sued me.

Ted: Crooks should be sued.

Rich: We paid.

Ted: Caroline Sweeney paid.

Rich: Two hundred million.

Ted: Her pop happy?

Rich: Tragic accident.

Ted: Pipeline checked?

Rich: Sure.

Ted: Report?

Rich: You bet.

Ted: No leaks?

Rich: Nothin'.

Ted: She smelled it often.

Rich: Says who?

Ted: Your people trained to lie.

Rich: Do their job.

Ted: Do the job all right.

Rich: Shit happens. Get over it.

Ted: Gotta live with that, Rich.

Rich: I paid.

Ted: Indians ripped off. Seventeen year-old girl burnt to cinders. Proud?

Rich: Sure.

Ted: Done with your life, Rich?

Rich: Forty billion dollars.

Ted: World ain't gonna forget Caroline Sweeney.

Rich: World ain't gonna forget Meyer Industries.

Ted: Or Stalin. World remembers evil.

Rich: Difference is we won.

Ted: Game's over?

Rich: World can't remember what it doesn't know.

Ted: In the papers, Rich.

Rich: Who pays attention?

Ted: The people.

Rich: The people know nothing.

Ted: People vote.

Rich: In blindfolds.

Ted: World changes.

Rich: Our way.

Ted: Can't control the people.

Rich: We do.

Ted: You're crazy.

Rich: Where'd they get their ideas?

Ted: First amendment.

Rich: Free speech for communists?

Ted: Democrats.

Rich: Tadpole becomes a frog, democrat becomes a communist.

Ted: Business gotta be honest.

Rich: Back to your wigwam.

Ted: What's America, Rich?

Rich: Business.

Ted: American flag means democracy.

Rich: Too much democracy.

Ted: People gonna say you're crazy.

Rich: People meddling. What you get? People gotta be told.

Ted: What to think?

Rich: Not to think.

Ted: Done with your life, bro?

Rich: Forty billion dollars.

BLACKOUT

Five seconds of silence. Out of the darkness:

Caroline (off): Pop. Smell it again, pop. Best tell someone. Hey, John. You comin'? John. Come on.

Engine starts and once more the auditorium is filled with the noise and light of an horrendous blast.

END

PARDON?

A play about, corruption, wealth, capitalism and the world's resources.

by
Alan Dent

CHARACTERS

George Marks, capitalist and fraudster.

Gunter Bamberg, banker.

Henry Black, Marks's business partner.

Saddam Hussein, the famous despot.

Daniel Franks, journalist.

Yitzhak Hankes, spy.

Daniella Marks, songwriter.

Karim Ali, Iranian government representative.

Dylan Harris, capitalist.

Bill Bray, lawyer.

Boris Volkov, Russian oligarch.

Sam Anderson, capitalist.

Matt Roe, lawyer.

Phil Kent, US Marshal.

The play is structured for 3 male actors and one female. Ideally, one scene segues seamlessly into the next.

SCENE ONE

An office. Atmosphere of wealth and power. George Marks, early thirties. Gunter Bamberg, early sixties.

Marks: Secret?
Bamberg: Natürlich.
Marks: Laws?
Bamberg: No problem.
Marks: Straight through Israel.
Bamberg: South to north.
Marks: North to south.
Bamberg: AC/DC.
They laugh.
Marks: Trade is trade.
Bamberg: Are we politicians?
Marks: Hitler needed bankers.
Bamberg: The world.
Marks: Who's squeamish?
Bamberg: I'm here.
Marks: Came through.
Bamberg: No choice.
Marks: They have no choice.
Bamberg: Rule the world.
Marks: So, the money.
Bamberg: Kein Problem.
Marks: My idea.
Bamberg: Yes?
Marks: Who needs capital?
Bamberg: Everybody. (Laughs)
Marks: Bank behind you, who knows?
Bamberg: Right.
Marks: Little capital, big profit.
Bamberg: Of course.

Marks: Iran.

Bamberg: Shah.

Marks: Our man.

Bamberg: Human conduit.

Marks: Sucks it in pisses it out.

They laugh.

Bamberg: Dictators are good for business.

Marks: Castro.

Bamberg: Needs oil.

Marks: Gaddafi.

Bamberg: Madman.

Marks: Buys stuff.

Bamberg: Sure.

Marks: Those guys.

Bamberg: Control.

Marks: Do business.

Bamberg: Have to.

Marks: Easy money.

Bamberg: We provide it.

Marks: I.G.Farben. Krupp.

Bamberg: Great.

Marks: That's money.

Bamberg: I was there.

Marks: Who cares?

Bamberg: Slave labour.

Marks: Profitable.

Bamberg: Next door to Auschwitz.

Marks: Best steel.

Bamberg: None better.

Marks: Krupp got prison.

Bamberg (with a shrug): Three years.

Marks: Too long.

Bamberg: Don't worry.

Marks: Too many laws.

Bamberg: Democracy.

Marks: The people.

Bamberg: Dummkopfen.

Marks: Oil is oil.

Bamberg: Let it flow.

Marks: I'll provide.

Bamberg: From?

Marks: Abadan.

Bamberg: To Eilat.

Marks: Round the Gulf.

Bamberg: Secretly?

Marks: Too many ships.

Bamberg: Careful.

Marks: Unload in secret.

Bamberg: Israeli supervision?

Marks: Mossad.

Bamberg: Wundebar.

Marks: How soon?

Bamberg: When you like.

Marks: No difficulty?

Bamberg: I run the bank.

Marks: Let's go.

Bamberg: Alles in Ordnung.

They shake hands.

BLACKOUT

SCENE TWO

A hotel room. Switzerland. Marks, forty. Henry Black, same age.

Marks: South Africa.

Black: Profitable?

Marks: Highly.

Black: Good regime.

Marks: Want oil, I sell them oil.

Black: Pinochet?

Marks: Easy.

Black: Angola?

Marks: Once war's over. Oil, diamonds.

Black: Marxists?

Marks: Marxists need oil.

Black: So, we set up.

Marks: We do.

Black: Capital?

Marks: Millions. South Africa. Good business.

Black: How'd you get in?

Marks: Learnt it at Peters. Tyranny is a good opportunity.

Black: No liberals.

Marks: Democracy gets in the way.

Black: Deal with the man in charge.

Marks: Got it.

Black: Know Pinochet?

Marks: Sure. Good guy.

Black: Big market?

Marks: Copper, nitrate.

Black: Unions?

Marks: Wiped 'em out.

Black: In on it?

Marks: What's good for nitrates?

Black: Agriculture.

Marks: War.

Black: Explosives.

Marks: There's war, we make millions.

Black: Let's have war. (They laugh).

Marks: Right.

Black: Where?

Marks: Africa, Asia, Latin America.

Black: Europe?

Marks: Too much democracy.

Blacks: The Balkans?

Marks: Always possible.

Black: Stir things up.

Marks: Like Vietnam.

Black: Liberals get in the way.

Marks: International law. UN. Bad for business.

Black: Copper?

Marks: Huge demand.

Black: Everywhere?

Marks: Cars, twenty to forty-five kilos.

Black: Wow.

Marks: Everyone on earth has a car, we're billionaires.

Black: Stuff run out?

Marks: We'll be dead.

Black: Carpe diem.

Marks: Building, electrics. Massive.

Black: Recycle the stuff?

Marks: Sure. Never enough.

Black; Gotta push up demand.

Marks: Got it.

Black: Everybody wants a car, a house.

Marks: People's wants, our profits.

Black: Shithole countries.

Marks: Big market.

Black: Wars, cars, building. We got it.

Marks: Stuff lies in the ground.

Black: It's ours.

Marks: Thousands o'years they been using copper.

Black: Sure.

Marks: Those primitives had no idea.

Black: Fortune under their feet.

Marks: Know what's funny?

Black: Uh-uh.

Marks: Coins.

Black: Copper.

Marks: Copper, alloys. Copper makes money, we smelt copper, we take the money.

Black: Nature's bounty.

Marks: Gotta grab it.

Black: By the pussy.

They laugh.

Marks: See the lawyers. Get this thing legal.

Black: Gonna call it?

Marks: George Marks and Co.

Black: Let's go.

BLACKOUT

SCENE THREE

Iraq. Plush surroundings. Marks and Saddam Hussein.

Marks: For the people.

Hussein: Iraqi people.

Marks: Great. Deal with the Russians?

Hussein: Good deal.

Marks: Terrific. What I'm saying.

Hussein: Yes.

Mark: Spot selling.

Hussein: Yes.

Marks: Why sell to the big guys?

Hussein: The Russians?

Marks: No, BP, Exxon.

Hussein: Do the business.

Marks: What I'm saying. Sell direct.

Hussein: Direct?

Marks: BP. Exxon. What they give you?

Hussein: Customers.

Marks: No. Customers are there. You sell to the big boys, they sell on.

Hussein: Your system.

Marks: Not mine.

Hussein: Capitalism.

Marks: Just means making money.

Hussein: BP. Exxon.

Marks: Sure. But I can do it.

Hussein: We sell to you, you sell on.

Marks: No. You sell to the customer. I provide the means.

Hussein: The means?

Marks: Sure. Financing, insurance, customs, so on.

Hussein: Nice for you.

Marks: And you.

Hussein: Iraq?

Marks: You too.

Hussein: For example.

Marks: Hundred thousand dollars.

Hussein: Quarter of a million.

Marks: Done.

They shake hands.

Hussein: Could be in trouble, Mr Marks.

Marks: Legal.

Hussein: Bribery ?

Marks: With foreigners.

Hussein: Your country is full of surprises.

Marks: Rules.

Hussein: Anarchist?

Marks: For losers. Contacts?

Hussein: With?

Marks: Nigeria.

Hussein: Gowon.

Marks: Good man?

Hussein: Crushes his enemies.

Marks: Some oil.

Hussein: Plenty.

Marks: I need an entry.

Hussein: I see.

Marks: Five percent.

Hussein: Ten.

Marks: Deal.

They shake hands.

Hussein: Talked to Brezhnev?

Marks: Not yet.

Hussein: Great man.

Marks: Yeah.

Hussein (taps forehead): Intellectual.

Marks: Interests me. States of Socialist Orientation.

Hussein: You're a capitalist.

Marks: I'm a businessman.

Hussein: Same.

Marks: Principles are for losers.

Hussein: Want to meet him?

Marks: Help him.

Hussein (taps forehead): Very shrewd.

Marks: You see, all those countries.

Hussein: Of socialist orientation.

Marks: Politics. I like making money.

Hussein: Poor countries.

Marks: Sure.

Hussein: Corrupt.

Marks: Corruption is good for business.

Hussein: Reward talent.

Marks: That's it.

Hussein: Need an entry.

Marks: The Soviets are in there.

Hussein: I'll see.

Marks: Soviet oil. Big.

Hussein: State control.

Marks: Sure, Like you. But they have to sell.

Hussein: Direct.

Marks: Got it.

Hussein: Okay.

Marks: I get rich. You get rich. The soviets get rich.

Hussein: The people's oil.

Marks: What do they know?

They laugh.

BLACKOUT

SCENE FOUR

Bar. Marks at table with Daniel Franks, journalist, 30.

Franks: Libya?
Marks: Sure.
Franks: Gaddafi as mad as they say?
Marks: Completely.
Franks laughs.
Franks: Business with the guy?
Marks: Bribery.
Franks laughs.
Franks: Yeah?
Marks: You bet.
Franks: Needs the dough.
Marks: Wealth stimulates greed.
Franks (writes): That's good.
Marks: Like sex.
Franks: Yeah?
Marks: More you have, more you want.
Franks: Right.
Marks: Never miss a chance.
Franks: Good. Venezuela?
Marks: Perez, good guy.
Franks: Oil nationalised.
Marks: Cares?
Franks: You in?
Marks: Billions.
Franks (writes): Terrific.
Marks: Oil keeps the people happy.
Franks: Course. Hospitals, schools.
Marks: Crumbs.
Franks: Exactly.

Marks: Price goes down, they're fucked.

Franks: You in trouble?

Marks: Gone.

Franks: Gets the blame?

Marks: Socialists.

Franks (writes): Terrific.

Marks: Don't print that.

Franks: Socialists in Venezuela?

Marks: Everywhere.

Franks: You mean, let 'em have power?

Marks: No need. Blame the workers.

Franks: Sure. But if they vote right?

Marks: Say they voted left.

Franks: Brilliant.

Marks: Your job.

Franks: Sure.

Marks: Get syndicated?

Franks: Sometimes.

Marks: Know what?

Franks: What?

Marks: The intellectuals.

Franks: Yeah?

Marks: They read the WSJ, FT. That shit.

Franks: They do.

Marks: Tempt the lions, they eat the antelopes.

Franks (writes): Very good.

Marks: Economist?

Franks: Yeah.

Marks: Books?

Franks: Not yet.

Marks: That's the thing.

Franks: Books?

Marks: Sure. Libraries.

Franks: Universities.

Marks: Right. Grab those ambitious kids.

Franks: Young.

Marks: Gotta read.

Franks; The right thing.

Marks: Spreads like measles.

Franks: Everybody gets it.

Marks: No inoculation.

Franks: Terrific. Castro?

Marks: Bribed him.

Franks (writes): Some socialist.

Marks: Can't beat the spot market.

Franks: Just oil?

Marks: Look.

Franks: Yeah?

Marks: Anything.

Franks: Really?

Marks: Name a commodity.

Franks: Coffee.

Marks: Drinks it?

Franks: Us.

Marks: Finns.

Franks: Kiddin'.

Marks: Rich countries.

Franks: Sure

Marks: Who grows it?

Franks: Poor countries.

Marks: Whose rules?

Franks: 'Course.

Marks: Futures.

Franks: Yeah.

Marks: Growers sell to Neumann, whoever.

Franks: Right.

Marks: Bang. Sell direct.

Franks: You do?

Marks: I will.

Franks: Competitive.

Marks: Competition is for losers.

Franks (writes): Lovely.

Marks: Monopoly is the only way. Another.

Franks: Sugar.

Marks: Seen the price?

Franks: Zoom!

Marks: Subsidies.

Franks: Ruin the market.

Marks: Worth tryin'. Another.

Franks: Rice.

Marks: Eats it?

Franks: Everybody.

Marks: The poor.

Franks: No meat.

Marks: Keeps billions alive.

Franks: Makes billions.

Marks: Control the staple, you win.

Franks (writes): Brilliant.

Marks: Gonna say about me?

Franks: Great businessman.

Marks: Bribery?

Franks: Legal.

Marks: It is.

Franks: Wampum.

Marks: Beads, oh boy.

Franks: Beavers.

Marks: Like a greasy beaver?

Franks: Love it.

Marks: Trade clam shells what you get?

Franks: Money.

Marks: What is money?

Franks: Life.

Marks: Like making money.

Franks: Genius for it.

Marks: Genius is the word.

Franks: Ceausescu?

Marks: Good guy.

Franks (writes) : Yeah?

Marks: Don't print that.

Franks: Oil, eh?

Marks: Refining. Embargo shot up the price.

Franks: Sell it?

Marks: Sure. Rotterdam spot.

Franks: Genius.

Marks: Executive President. Makes it easy.

Franks: Know who you're dealin' with.

Marks: Exactly. No democratic shit.

Franks: Democracy muddles everything.

Marks: Securitate. Gets things done.

Franks: Hospitals, Psychiatric prisons.

Marks: Shut the big mouths.

Franks: Likes capitalism?

Marks: Money. Power.

Franks: Same thing

Marks: Marxist theory, capitalist practice.

Franks: Great mix.

Marks: Sure. Keep the people quiet. Make money.

Franks: Genius.

Marks: Enough?

Franks: Sure.

Marks (as they shake hands): Say nice things.

Franks: You bet.

BLACKOUT

SCENE FIVE

Office. Marks and Yitzhak Hankes, spy.

Hankes: Netherlands, USA, Portugal, South Africa..
Marks (nods): Revenge.
Hankes: Nixon.
Marks: Gold Standard?
Hankes: Big losses.
Marks: In trouble?
Hankes: Soon.
Marks: Months?
Hankes: Weeks.
Marks: Weeks?
Hankes: Can't get it.
Marks: Eilat-Ashkelon?
Hankes: Empty.
Marks: Don't worry.
Hankes: From?
Marks: Iran.
Hankes: Contacts?
Marks: Enough.
Hankes: They get?
Marks: Weapons.
Hankes: Unreliable.
Marks: Small stuff.
Hankes: Dunno.
Marks: The IDF! The Shah.
Hankes: I know. But Arabs.
Marks: Nukes.
Hankes: Maybe.
Marks: No need to be coy.
Hankes: Don't say, no one knows.
Marks: I know.

Hankes: Iran.

Marks: Get oil.

Hankes: Yom Kippur nearly did for us.

Marks: US bodyguard.

Hankes: Sure. But.

Marks: Gotta bribe.

Hankes: Money?

Marks: Spend it on?

Hankes: Cares.

Marks: Weapons?

Hankes: Dunno.

Marks: No oil, no Israel.

Hankes: Know the Shah?

Marks: Nearly.

Hankes: Intelligence?

Marks: Sure.

Hankes: Good people?

Marks: Bribed.

Hankes: On our side?

Marks: Question of money.

Hankes: Shah thinks he's god.

Marks: Thinks he's a socialist.

Hankes: Sex five times a day.

Marks: Plenty on him?

Hankes: Trying to outdo the west.

Marks: Let him.

Hankes: Religious elite don't like it.

Marks: Tough.

Hankes: He falls.

Marks: No chance.

Hankes: Another attempt on his life.

Marks: He dies. So what? You get oil.

Hankes: Okay. Soon?

Marks: Tankers ready.

Hankes: Plenty?

Marks: Embargo was inevitable. I bought up.

Hankes: Not my decision.

Marks: Sure.

Hankes: Let you know.

Marks: Soon.

Hankes: Soon.

They shake hands.

BLACKOUT

SCENE SIX

Living-room. Atmosphere of great wealth. Marks, 40 and Daniella, his wife, 30.

Daniella (as Marks reads): You think?

Marks: Good.

Daniella: I know. How good?

Marks: Very.

Daniella: Number one?

Marks: Sure.

Daniella: You know business.

Marks: You asked.

Daniella: Moral support.

Marks: Try it.

Daniella: Competition's cruel.

Marks: Murder it.

Daniella: Got a hit man?

Marks: Plenty.

Daniella: Russian?

Marks: Sure.

Daniella: Guy doin' ?

Marks: Black market.

Daniella: Lucrative?

Marks: Pretty.

Daniella: Into oil?

Marks: No. Maybe get him to America.

Daniella: Jackson-Vanik?

Marks: Sure.

Daniella: Got a deal with Russia?

Marks: Yeah.

.

Daniella: Doin' well?

Marks: Sure.

Daniella: What else?

Marks: Iran.

Daniella: Muslims?

Marks: Rich Muslims.

Daniella: Rakin' it?

Marks: Course.

Daniella: Fund my music.

Marks: Buy you in.

Daniella: Pay for this (waves paper).

Marks: No trouble.

Daniella: One hit, I'm launched.

Marks: We'll do it.

Daniella: Hear it again?

Marks: You like.

She sings a sentimental 70s style pop song.

Daniella: The lyric?

Marks: Perfect.

Daniella: The refrain is okay?

Marks: Fine.

Daniella: Know any producers?

Marks: No.

Daniella: Find some?

Marks: Sure.

Daniella: Way in.

Marks: I know.

Daniella: One hit is a wave.

Marks: Ride it.

Daniella: For years.

Marks: Life.

Daniella: Buy a label.

Marks: Maybe.

Daniella: Big.

Marks: Only big is worth it.

Daniella: Fox.

Marks: Not for sale.

Daniella: Bid.
Marks: I know business.
Daniella: For me.
Marks: One day.
Daniella (sits on his knee): One day? Honey.
Marks: I know business.
Daniella: I know?
Marks: You know.
Daniella: For me.

BLACKOUT

SCENE SEVEN

Office. Marks and Karim Ali, Iranian.

Ali: How much?
Marks: As you like.
Ali: Hostages?
Marks: Politics.
Ali: Prison.
Marks: Catch me.
Ali: Carter says terrorism.
Marks (shrugs): Carter.
Ali: Ayatollah respects agreements.
Marks: Good man.
Ali: Carter said the Shah was beloved.
Marks: Who cares?
Ali: Your opinion?
Marks: No opinion.
Ali: Fifty-two Americans.
Marks: I'm neutral.
Ali: You're American
Marks: Business is neutral.
Ali: Humiliating.
Marks: For America.
Ali: For you.
Marks: I'm not America.
Ali: Americans are angry.
Marks: Not me.
Ali: Americans like sanctions.
Marks: Let 'em.
Ali: Sixty million barrels?
Marks: Sure.
Ali: Who'll buy.
Marks: South Africa, Israel.

Ali: Israel?

Marks: Need oil.

Ali: The Ayatollah doesn't like Israel.

Marks: Israel doesn't like him. So what? It's business.

Ali: Your sympathies?

Marks: None.

Ali: All have sympathies.

Marks: Money.

Ali: Breaking embargoes. Long prison sentence.

Marks: I'll worry.

Ali: Do it?

Marks: Shell companies, fixers, bribes.

Ali: Fixers might tell.

Marks: Why?

Ali: People boast.

Marks: People like money.

Ali: People like rules.

Marks: Ayatollah?

Ali: Strict rules.

Marks: Breaks 'em.

Ali: Got to sell oil.

Marks: Business.

Ali: Okay. Sixty million barrels minimum.

Marks: Done.

Ali: FBI finds out, don't come to us.

Marks: Somewhere nice.

Ali: Yes?

Marks: Tax haven. Some offshore place.

Ali: Find you.

Marks: Can't touch me if it's legal.

Ali: Not legal in America.

Marks: Law. Democracy. Bullshit. I'm a businessman.

BLACKOUT

SCENE EIGHT

Office. Marks, smoking cigar and Dylan Harris, oil man, slick capitalist, eating throughout.

Harris: Other people's money.
Marks: No risk.
Harris: Unlimited credit.
Marks: Hushed.
Harris: Not a word.
Marks: When they knew, too late.
Harris: Look at the pretty girl.
Marks: Everyone thinks.
Harris: Poker.
Marks: What to keep?
Harris: Movies.
Marks: Never love an asset.
Harris: Never love anything.
They laugh.
Marks: Janet.
Harris: One thing.
Marks: What to sell?
Harris: Met Lucille Ball?
Marks: Nope.
Harris: Hear a joke?
Marks: Yeah.
Harris: Was it? Guy goes into a brothel…
Marks: She told it?
Harris: She did. Guy goes into a brothel and says…
Marks: One funny woman.
Harris: Woody Allen?
Marks: No.
Harris: Funniest guy.
Marks: Sell the golf courses?

Harris: Maybe. Jack Lemmon?

Marks: No.

Harris: Allen, Lemmon, sad looking guys.

Marks: Guess.

Harris: Laugh. Was it? Guy goes into a brothel and says, "I'd like a red-head…"

Marks: Movies make money.

Harris: Some. Love 'em.

Marks: Never love what you sell.

Harris: Ginger Rogers?

Marks: No.

Harris: *Monkey Business*?

Marks: Funny.

Harris: Hilarious. Genius. One of ours.

Marks: Hit.

Harris: Cary Grant?

Marks: No.

Harris: Shook his hand.

Marks: Yeah. Sell the drinks?

Harris: Maybe. Gregory Peck?

Marks: No.

Harris: Charming.

Marks: Liberal.

Harris: No power.

Marks: Vietnam.

Harris: *Spellbound*?

Marks: No.

Harris: See it.

Marks: Yeah?

Harris: Bergman. Terrific.

Marks: Met her?

Harris: No. Guy goes into a brothel…

Marks: Greenmailing?

Harris: Who?

Marks: Whoever.

Harris: Maybe.

Marks: Old oil as new.

Harris (laughs): FBI runnin' round on amphetamines.

Marks: Fine.

Harris: $20,000. Peanuts.

Marks: Price o' doin' business.

Harris: Reagan said?

Marks: What?

Harris: Too much sex.

Marks: Possible?

Harris: Copy Lubitsch.

Marks: Who?

Harris: I said.

Marks: Sex sells.

Harris: Sex is business.

Marks: Life is business.

Harris: The movies. Love 'em.

Marks: Gotta sell somethin'.

Harris: Sure.

Marks: Bottling plant.

Harris: Maybe.

Marks: What good's a bottling plant?

Harris: You like soda?

Marks: Made for stripping.

Harris: Okay. Bottling plant.

Marks: Music publishing.

Harris: Dick Van Dyke?

Marks: No.

Harris: Funny guy.

Marks: Sure.

Harris: *Bye Bye Birdie*?

Marks: No.

Harris: Genius. Based on Presley.

Marks: Yeah.

Harris: Like him?

Marks: Okay.

Harris: Genius.

Marks: Music publishing?

Harris: Sure.

Marks: Quick profit.

Harris: Right.

Marks: Movie theatres in Australia.

Harris: I like movies.

Marks: Assets are money.

Harris: Okay.

Marks: Strip 'em.

Harris: Maybe.

Marks: Real estate.

Harris: Bob Hope?

Marks: No.

Harris: *Eight on the Lam*?

Marks: Heard of it.

Harris: Funny guy.

Marks: Sure.

Harris: Genius.

Marks: So, the real estate?

Harris: No panic.

Marks: Losing money.

Harris: Not ours.

Marks: Need a gusher.

Harris: What we put in?

Marks: Fifty million?

Harris: Assets back the loans, not us.

Marks: Sure. But all this stuff.

Harris: Yeah, strip it.

Marks: All of it?

Harris: Strip it.

Marks: Good.

Harris: Know what?

Marks: Yeah?

Harris: Oil man, no one knew me.

Marks: Who cares?

Harris: Now any restaurant in Hollywood, I'm in.

Marks: Okay.

Harris: Kissinger, Ford, everybody.

Marks: Okay.

Harris: Movies. Love 'em.

Marks: We strip?

Harris: We do.

BLACKOUT

SCENE NINE

Office. Marks and Bill Bray, his lawyer.

Bray: Sixty-five.
Marks: Defence?
Bray: Tough.
Marks: All of 'em?
Bray: Fraud, racketeering, oil from Iran…
Marks: So?
Bray: Leave the country.
Marks: How long?
Bray: Tomorrow.
Marks: Hold 'em off.
Bray: Serious charges, George.
Marks: Tomorrow?
Bray: Today if possible.
Marks: Where?
Bray: Anywhere with no extradition.
Marks: London?
Bray: Sorry.
Marks: Big city.
Bray: One phone call.
Marks: Lie low?
Bray: Money?
Marks: Joking?
Bray: Stay in business?
Marks: Sure.
Bray: Not in London.
Marks: Paris?
Bray: Brunei.
Marks: Nice place?
Bray: Lovely.
Marks: Remind me.

Bray: Borneo.
Marks: Temperate?
Bray: Natives call it Kalamanthana.
Marks: Nice.
Bray: Burning weather.
Marks: Resources?
Bray: Rain forest, oil.
Marks: Logging?
Bray: Orangutans.
Marks: Protected?
Bray: You know oil.
Marks: Runs it?
Bray: The Sultan.
Marks: Amenable?
Bray: Absolutist.
Marks: Makes things easy.
Bray: If he likes you.
Marks: Where else?
Bray: Vanuatu.
Marks: My geography.
Bray: South Pacific.
Marks: Interesting?
Bray: Wreck of Coolidge.
Marks: Didn't bury him?
Bray: Ship.
Marks: Okay.
Bray: Land diving.
Marks: Dangerous?
Bray: Try it?
Marks: Germany?
Bray: Forget it.
Marks: Europe.
Bray: Vatican City.
Marks: Catholic?

Bray: Convert.

Marks: Jewish catholic?

Bray: Mongrels are interesting.

Marks: Latin?

Bray: Wanna read encyclicals?

Marks: Lives there?

Bray: Most Popes per square kilometre.

Marks: And?

Bray: Eight hundred and twenty-four others.

Marks: Women?

Bray: Few. High crime rate.

Marks: Catholics are criminals?

Bray: It's said. Tourists.

Marks: Cops?

Bray: Their own. Not in the UN.

Marks: Don't say. Where else?

Bray: Saudi.

Marks: Okay. Oil.

Bray: Plenty.

Marks: King Fahd.

Bray: Right.

Marks: Absolutist.

Bray: No elections, no liberals.

Marks: Makes life easy.

Bray: No booze.

Marks: Legally.

Bray: Correct.

Marks: Not much fun for Daniella.

Bray: Public executions.

Marks: Not if you're the victim.

Bray: She faithful.

Marks: Impertinence.

Bray: Cape Verde?

Marks: Remote?

Bray: Eight hundred kilometres from Africa.
Marks: Oil?
Bray: No.
Marks: Coffee?
Bray: No.
Marks: Rice?
Bray: No.
Marks: Gold?
Bray: No.
Marks: What?
Bray: Limestone.
Marks: Wow.
Bray: Parliamentary democracy.
Marks: In Africa?
Bray: Sure.
Marks: What happened?
Bray: They had a revolt.
Marks: Against the Portugese.
Bray. Right.
Marks: Make a living there?
Bray: Tourism.
Marks: And limestone.
Bray: Nice climate.
Marks: Cute.
Bray: And birds.
Marks: Switzerland?
Bray: Possible.
Marks: Civilised.
Bray: Democratic.
Marks: Not the banks.
Bray: Direct democracy.
Marks: Not the banks.
Bray: Most corrupt in the world.
Marks: Country's rich.

Bray: Richest.

Marks: Corruption works.

Bray: Bank for International Settlements.

Marks: My kinda bank.

Bray: Gold to the Nazis.

Marks: Business.

Bray: Jew.

Marks: Businessman.

Bray: Jewish businessman or businessman who's Jewish?

Marks: Business has no religion.

Bray: Ethnicity?

Marks: No. I like skiing.

Bray: Chocolate?

Marks: Bern? Geneva?

Bray: Come for you.

Marks: Lie low.

Bray: And do business?

Marks: Money is a shape-shifter.

Bray: Need more beds than Arafat.

Marks: Disguise. Move around.

Bray: Okay.

Marks: When?

Bray: Now.

Marks: Tomorrow.

Bray: They come tonight?

Marks: Well guarded.

Bray: Okay. Tomorrow.

BLACKOUT

SCENE TEN

Hotel room, plush. Marks and Daniella. Marks on landline.

Marks: A steal.
Harris: Sure.
Marks: Hundred and fifteen million.
Harris: Hand has the teeth marks. (Laughs).
Marks: Six times less than we paid.
Harris: Ain't business wonderful? (Laughs).
Marks: Government screwed me.
Harris: Government's screw everybody. Bogart?
Marks: No.
Harris: Genius. *In A Lonely Place*?
Marks: No.
Harris: Bogart is Dix Steele.
Marks: Government got my money.
Harris: Everybody's money. Hat girl is murdered.
Marks: Yeah?
Harris: Dix suspected.
Marks: Government robs me you rob the government.
Harris: Merry go round. (Laughs). What's the motive?
Marks: Who's?
Harris: Dix.
Marks: Dix?
Harris: Film.
Marks: Like it back.
Harris: Violent guy.
Marks: Who?
Harris Dix.
Daniella who is pacing, singing to herself, shows him what she's writing. He nods. Smiles. She carries on.
Marks: Criminal.
Harris: Who?

162

Marks: Government.
Harris: Gangsters. Scares Laurel.
Marks: Who?
Harris: Dix.
Marks: Laurel?
Harris: Neighbour.
Marks: I'm on the lam?
Harris: Crashes.
Marks: What?
Harris: The car.
Marks: Who?
Harris: Dix.
Marks: What I do?
Harris: Nearly kills the guy.
Marks: What guy?
Harris: Driver.
Marks: Dix?
Harris: Other.
Marks: Victim.
Harris: Who?
Marks: Me.
Harris: Innocent.
Marks: I am.
Harris: What?
Marks: Innocent.
Harris: Dix.
Marks: Nearly killed the guy.
Harris: Driver.
Marks: Yeah.
Harris: Not the hat girl.
Marks: Who?
Harris: The hat girl. Murdered.
Marks: Who?
Harris: Husband.

Daniella shows Harris the paper again. He nods. Smiles. She carries on.

Marks: Hundreds o' millions.

Harris: Who?

Marks: Government.

Harris: Communists.

Marks: Bargain.

Harris: Man loses another gains. Gloria Swanson?

Marks: No.

Harris: *Sunset Boulevard*?

Marks: I think.

Harris: Genius. William Holden?

Marks: No.

Harris: Guy.

Marks: Gonna do with it?

Harris: What?

Marks: My share?

Harris: Joe Gillis. Dead in pool.

Marks: What pool?

Harris: Hers.

Marks: Whose?

Harris: Norma Desmond.

Marks: Norma Desmond?

Harris: Gloria Swanson.

Marks: Killed him?

Harris: She did.

Marks: Gloria Swanson?

Harris: Norma Desmond.

Marks: Why?

Harris: Fantasy.

Marks: Gonna do with it?

Harris: Sell it. Isotta Faschini?

Marks: Who?

Harris: Car.

Marks: Oh, yeah.
Harris: Bette Davis?
Marks: No.
Harris: Genius.
Daniella shows Harris the paper. He nods, smiles. She carries on.
Marks: How much?
Harris: Who knows? *All About Eve*?
Marks: Yeah.
Harris: Eve Harrington. Star struck.
Marks: Two Hundred?
Harris: Your share?
Marks: Yeah.
Harris: Marilyn Monroe.
Marks: What?
Harris: Unknown.
Marks: Monroe is unknown?
Harris: Was. Everybody loves a star.
Marks: Robbed.
Harris: Two fifty.
Marks: Who?
Harris: Who bids.
Marks: My assets.
Harris: *Three Little Words*?
Marks: Which?
Harris: Astaire.
Marks: Start from scratch.
Harris: Nothing?
Marks: Well, some.
Harris: Genius.
Marks: Government?
Harris: Astaire.
Marks: Who needs government?
Harris: Losers. *Kiss Tomorrow Goodbye*?

Daniella shows him the paper, starts to sing notes of a trite melody. He nods. Smiles.
Marks: No.

BLACKOUT

SCENE ELEVEN

Office, Switzerland. Marks and Boris Volkov, 35, capitalist.

Marks: Most profitable.
Volkov: Yeah?
Marks: Apartheid. Simple.
Volkov: Sure.
Marks: Coal. The traders profit, the miners lose.
Volkov: World works.
Marks: Did great.
Volkov: Thanks.
Marks: Best analyst.
Volkov: Work hard.
Marks: Our strong man.
Volkov: Gotta win.
Marks: Still running?
Volkov: Every day.
Marks: Winner.
Volkov: Gotta be.
Marks: Hong Kong. Brilliant work.
Volkov: Easy.
Marks: Sure. No liberals.
Volkov: No unions.
Marks: Crucial.
Volkov: So, coal.
Marks: Head of division.
Volkov: Fine.
Marks: Manipulate the market.
Volkov: Like South Africa.
Marks: Sure. China, big player.
Volkov: Dictatorship makes certainty.
Marks: Exactly. Billions.
Volkov: No failure.

Marks: Markets. Up and down.

Volkov: Failure is impossible.

Marks: Avoidable.

Volkov: I'm rich.

Marks: Get richer.

Volkov: Lose money I'll be rich. But failure.

Marks: Business is roulette.

Volkov: Fix the wheel.

Marks: Okay. Your success, our profit.

Volkov: Okay. Free hand?

Marks: Course.

Volkov: One thing.

Marks: Yeah?

Volkov: Anyone fails. They're out.

Marks: Free hand.

Volkov: Let's go.

BLACKOUT

SCENE TWELVE

Same office. Marks and Sam Anderson, 40, capitalist.

Anderson: One thousand four hundred per metric tonne.
Marks: Yeah.
Anderson: We buy one million.
Marks: One million?
Anderson: Sure.
Marks: Goes down?
Anderson: Twenty per cent of global.
Marks: Eighty per cent not ours.
Anderson: Twenty per cent, we hold it.
Marks: Yeah?
Anderson: Shortage.
Marks: Eighty per cent available.
Anderson: Twenty per cent enough.
Marks: I dunno.
Anderson: China.
Marks: Yeah?
Anderson: Happening?
Marks: Communism.
Anderson: Capitalism. Cities like cancer cells.
Marks: Okay.
Anderson: Cities grow, zinc is water.
Marks: Right.
Anderson: Twenty per cent of global and we don't sell.
Marks: Price goes up.
Anderson: Push me, pull you.
Marks: One million at one thousand four hundred.
Anderson: Exactly.
Marks: Lotta dough.
Anderson: Money for?
Marks: I know.

Anderson: Shortage is yeast.

Marks: Sure. But eighty per cent.

Anderson: Think. You're in China.

Marks: Yeah.

Anderson: Hear zinc is getting scarce.

Marks: Eighty per cent is scarce?

Anderson: Twenty per cent is our hand on their balls.

Marks: How much?

Anderson: Think. A hundred dollars. We have a million tonnes.

Marks: Okay. Think. It falls twenty dollars. We have a million tonnes.

Anderson: Talking like a socialist.

Marks: Roulette.

Anderson: Pessimism.

Marks: Caution.

Anderson: Caution made you Rich?

Marks: Control.

Anderson: Twenty per cent is control.

Marks: Eighty per cent is control.

Anderson: Twenty per cent we control.

Marks: Eighty per cent we don't.

Anderson: Bound to rise.

Marks: Sure to fall.

Anderson: After.

Marks: One thousand four hundred. High.

Anderson: Pull twenty per cent. Higher.

Marks: Ceiling.

Anderson: Knows?

Marks: One thousand four hundred. Phew.

Anderson: Our share. Clamour.

Marks: Knows?

Anderson: One dollar, one million.

Marks: Ten dollars ten million.

Anderson: Right.

Marks: Down.

Anderson: Won't happen.

Marks: 1939.

Anderson: Pessimism.

Marks: Never will happen.

Anderson: Pessimism built America?

Marks: Control.

Anderson: Corner the market.

Marks: Manipulate.

Anderson: Right.

Marks: Twenty per cent?

Anderson: No bet no win.

Marks: Ten per cent.

Anderson: Control?

Marks: Odds?

Anderson: Five to one.

Marks: Our favour?

Anderson: Sure.

Marks: Prefer twenty.

Anderson: The wheel turns.

Marks: We lose.

Anderson: Hand on their balls.

Marks: Cut 'em off.

Anderson: Wish.

Marks: Control. Certainty.

Anderson: I know.

Marks: Volkov?

Anderson: Yeah.

Marks: Totally?

Anderson: Thinks.

Marks: Smart.

Anderson: Very.

Marks: Thinks?

Anderson: Does.
Marks: Twenty?
Anderson: Twenty.
Marks: Okay.
Anderson: Today.
Marks: Sure. But.
Anderson: Yeah?
Marks: Up, we sell.
Anderson: How much?
Marks: Ask Volkov.
Anderson: Okay.

BLACKOUT

SCENE THIRTEEN

Same office. Marks and Volkov.

Volkov: One thousand and fifty.
Marks: And fifty?
Volkov: Four hundred million.
Marks: Sold?
Volkov: Most.
Marks: Anderson?
Volkov: Yeah.
Marks: Four hundred?
Volkov: At least.
Marks: Ride it.
Volkov: The boys.
Marks: Yeah?
Volkov: Your share.
Marks: Listen.
Volkov: Majority stake.
Marks: My company.
Volkov: Business.
Marks: Ride it.
Volkov: Four hundred.
Marks: Pull it back.
Volkov: Sure. But.
Marks: Yeah?
Volkov: Failure.
Marks: One mistake.
Volkov: Wipe us out.
Marks: No.
Volkov: Nearly.
Marks: Anderson.
Volkov: Bad bet.
Marks: I said. Control.

Volkov: Correct.

Marks: Twenty per cent. He said twenty per cent.

Volkov: Hand on their balls.

Marks: Didn't squeeze hard enough.

Volkov: The boys.

Marks: My share?

Volkov: Yeah.

Marks: Still in?

Volkov: Sure.

Marks: Minority?

Volkov: Right.

Marks: You and me.

Volkov: You and me?

Marks: Pull it round.

Volkov: Failure.

Marks: Setback.

Volkov: Don't like it.

Marks: Make money.

Volkov: Yeah.

Marks: Stick together.

Volkov: Can't stand failure.

Marks: Few years. Back on top.

Volkov: Failure is failure.

Marks: The boys?

Volkov: Yeah.

 Pardon ? Dent. Page 48.

Marks: Agree?

Volkov: Have to.

Marks: My company.

Volkov: Not any more.

BLACKOUT

SCENE FOURTEEN

Paris. Hotel room. Hankes and Matt Roe, 50, lawyer.

Roe: Some city.
Hankes; Beautiful.
Roe: Beautiful. Jules Verne?
Hankes: No.
Roe: Must.
Hankes: Yeah.
Roe: Dinner.
Hankes; Book.
Roe: We will. Working for Marks.
Hankes: Working? Paid.
Roe: Good. Spying?
Hankes: Retired.
Roe: Spies retire?
Hankes: Always alert.
Roe: The donation. Thanks.
Hankes: Pleasure.
Roe: Do something for Marks.
Hankes: Should.
Roe: President.
Hankes: Know him?
Roe: Indirectly.
Hankes: Weak?
Roe: Persuadable.
Hankes: Plenty on him.
Roe: Not that.
Hankes: No?
Roe: Compassion.
Hankes: You think?
Roe: Sure. Liberal.

Hankes: Tax fraud.

Roe: Long gone.

Hankes: Who?

Roe: Daniella.

Hankes: Knows him?

Roe: Donations.

Hankes: Neat.

Roe: Two hundred and fifty thousand.

Hankes: To?

Roe: Library, arts, this, that.

Hankes: She will?

Roe: Persuade her.

Hankes: Me?

Roe: Right background.

Hankes: Just her?

Roe: No. Get a list.

Hankes: Who?

Roe: Eminent. Profs, Nobel laureates, ex-Prime Ministers…

Hankes: In person?

Roe: Letters.

Hankes: You think?

Roe: Sure. Enough will shift him.

Hankes: Presidential pardon?

Roe: That's it.

Hankes: Good man. Philanthropist. Dues paid.

Roe: Got it.

Hankes: Okay.

Roe: Put you in touch.

Hankes: Fine.

Roe: Dinner.

Hankes: Let's go.

SCENE FIFTEEN

Office. Downbeat, untidy, small. Atmosphere of reduced resources. Phil Kent, Marshal on mobile.

Kent: Smoking gun is greed.
Director (off as for rest of scene): You got, Phil?
Kent: Brick wall, boss.
Director: Location?
Kent: Sure.
Director: Get him.
Kent: Last time.
Director: Yeah?
Kent: Fancy restaurant.
Director: Had him?
Kent: Men's room window.
Director: No kiddin'?
Kent: I can make a thousand mistakes, he can't make one.
Director: Doesn't?
Kent: Not yet.
Director: Contacts?
Kent: Dozens. Thirty-three countries.
Director: Gets around.
Kent: Tell you.
Director: Yeah?
Kent: Queuein' up to squeal.
Director: Popular guy.
Kent: Screwed everybody.
Director: All the evidence you need.
Kent: Yeah, not him.
Director: Who's protecting?
Kent: Presidents. Prime Ministers. Finance ministers.
Director: Where?
Kent: Name it.

Director: North Korea.

Kent: Yep. Through the Russians.

Director: Communists like him?

Kent: Greedy like him.

Director: Stop his money.

Kent: Two million in cash in a suitcase to London.

Director: Got it?

Kent: Customs.

Director: For?

Kent: Which oil minister was in London?

Director: Someone behind bars want him brought low?

Kent: Know what Ivanov told me?

Director: Yeah?

Kent: Very few people in the world can lend one another a billion, no questions.

Director: Ivanov got the dirt?

Kent: Banks ripped him off.

Director: Insider trading?

Kent: Leverage. Arbitrage. What's the little guy know?

Director: Knows Ivanov is a crook.

Kent: A rich crook.

Director: With a record.

Kent: He cares.

Director: Do what we can.

Kent: Law's a beach hut, money's a tsunami.

Director: Man made a lot of enemies.

Kent: And friends. Buys heads of state.

Director: Weak point?

Pardon ? Dent. Page 54.

Kent: Strength of this man in the world economy. Countries got nothin' on him.

Director: Arrest somebody.

Kent: Remember the Venezuelan?

Director: Remind me.

Kent: Ex-President and his woman.

Director: Yeah.

Kent: Expired visa.

Director. I know.

Kent: Had 'em.

Director: She was the conduit.

Kent: To the government.

Director: INS told by the Embassy to release 'em.

Kent: Right.

Director: Find out why?

Kent: No. But I know.

Director: His people?

Kent: Like staring into a black hole.

Director: Gotta co-operate. We fund 'em.

Kent: Love him. Charitable. Benefactor of humanity.

Director: Believe that?

Kent: What they say.

Director: Russians want revenge?

Kent: Kleptocrats love kleptocrats. Trained 'em in fraud, kickbacks, shell companies, Swiss accounts, banks in the Caymans.

Director: Looted their wealth.

Kent: Sure. The rich care?

Director: One mistake.

Kent: Sly.

Director: Sure.

Kent: Bid to mine the Amazon failed, what's he do?

Director: I know. Funds environmental group.

Kent: Competitor loses contract, he bids at half the going rate and pulls the dollars from the greens.

Director: One mistake.

Kent: Yeah. Greed is the smoking gun.

Director: Greed will betray him.

Kent: Not his. Politicians with commodities.

Director: Way to go, Phil.
Kent: Okay.

BLACKOUT

SCENE SIXTEEN

Office. Marks and Roe.

Marks: Prejudice.
Roe: You think?
Marks: Sure. Everywhere.
Roe: Right.
Marks: I do?
Roe: Above board?
Marks: It's business.
Roe: Sure.
Marks: Jungle.
Roe: Naturally.
Marks: Nice guys make money?
Roe: I know.
Marks: How much've I given?
Roe: Quarter of a million.
Marks: Double it.
Roe: Thank you.
Marks: I'm a bad guy?
Roe: Support good causes.
Marks: Prejudice.
Roe: Maybe.
Marks: Who gives to charity?
Roe: Everybody.
Marks: Ten dollars. Who cares.
Roe: Ten dollars and ten dollars and ten dollars.
Marks: Sure. But who gives big?
Roe: The rich.
Marks: Who gets rich?
Roe: Smart guys.
Marks: Bend the rules here. Cheat there.
Roe: I know.

Marks: I'm a criminal?

Roe: They say.

Marks: Who says?

Roe: The law.

Marks: Law is for little guys.

Roe: Democracy.

Marks: Too much democracy.

Roe: Sure.

Marks: Business in chains.

Roe: I know.

Marks: Are we the people?

Roe: Right.

Marks: Chain the best people?

Roe: You're right.

Marks: Our people.

Roe: The best.

Marks: You can pick it up.

Roe: Need evidence.

Marks: Evidence?

Roe: I say this, that. People will say. Evidence?

Marks: I'm climbing through bathroom windows to escape Marshalls.

Roe: They'll say. The law.

Marks: Everybody breaks the law.

Roe: I know.

Marks: Counts is winning.

Roe: Taxes.

Marks: Who likes 'em?

Roe: Sure.

Marks: Taxation is the ruination of business.

Roe: Got a point.

Marks: State for?

Roe: Defence.

Marks: Correct. One thing. Defend property.

Roe: Essentially.

Marks: Completely. Education. Healthcare. Roads. Garbage collection. No. Property.

Roe: Gotta educate kids, George.

Marks: I should pay?

Roe: We all pay.

Marks: What's that?

Roe: Democracy.

Marks: Communism.

Roe: Liberalism.

Marks: Same. Prejudice.

Roe: Falling.

Marks: What?

Roe: Prejudice.

Marks: Giving up?

Roe: Eternal vigilance.

Marks: Falling?

Roe: Fact.

Marks: Everywhere.

Roe: But falling.

Marks: Says who?

Roe: Surveys.

Marks: Believe 'em?

Roe: Officially obliterated.

Marks: Obliterated?

Roe: Sure.

Marks: Officialdom is with our people?

Roe: Not against.

Marks: Look. My case.

Roe: I know.

Marks: Prejudice.

Roe: Breaking embargoes, George.

Marks: Everybody breaks embargoes.

Roe: Iran.

Marks: Business.

Roe: Sure. But our people.

Marks: Business first, Matt.

Roe: I know.

Marks: Make a case.

Roe: Difficult.

Marks: Difficult? They object, it's prejudice.

Roe: Sure. But a pardon.

Marks: Do that?

Roe: Daniella.

Marks: Yeah?

Roe: They say divorce makes couples more friendly.

Marks: Okay.

Roe: We'll try.

Marks: How?

Roe: She writes the President.

Marks: He knows her?

Roe: Of her.

Marks: One letter.

Roe: Hundreds.

Marks: From her.

Roe: Got a list.

Marks: Yeah.

Roe: Long.

Marks: Example?

Roe: Joe Warwick.

Marks: Who?

Roe: History professor.

Marks: Where?

Roe: Yale.

Marks: With us?

Roe He is.

Marks: Why?

Roe: Our people.

Marks: Okay. That's two.

Roe: Austin May.

Marks: Prof?

Roe: Physicist.

Marks: Famous?

Roe: Influential.

Marks: Our people?

Roe: Uh-uh.

Marks: Three.

Roe: Laura Bellini.

Marks: She?

Roe: Writer.

Marks: Good?

Roe: Nobel.

Marks: Don't say?

Roe: She is.

Marks: Read her?

Roe: Nope.

Marks: And?

Roe: Brian Swire.

Marks: Swire?

Roe: Ex-Prime Minister.

Marks: Of?

Roe: Somewhere.

Marks: Our people?

Roe: Right.

Marks: President know him?

Roe; Met him.

Marks: Buddies.

Roe: Presidents meet people. Shake hands. How ya doin'?

Marks: Celebs?

Roe: Stella Baker.

Marks: Yeah?

Roe: Sure.

Marks: Like her?

Roe: Handsome woman.

Marks: Her singing.

Roe: I can listen.

Marks: President?

Roe: Handsome woman.

Marks: Got the eye.

Roe: Got the balls.

Marks: Done her?

Roe: Who knows?

Marks: That it?

Roe: Ed Fallon.

Marks: Famous?

Roe: Economist.

Marks: President know him?

Roe: Adviser.

Marks: Okay. Who else?

Roe: Plenty.

Marks: Daniella? You think?

Roe: Sure.

Marks: I talk to her ?

Roe: Me.

Marks: She says no?

Roe: Persuasion.

Marks: Like?

Roe: Singing stuff.

Marks: Know people?

Roe: People can be bought.

Marks: Okay. I'm innocent.

Roe: I know.

Marks: Prejudice.

Roe: Get the pardon, who cares?

Marks: Doesn't bend the rules?

Roe: Losers.

Marks: Right.

BLACKOUT

SCENE SEVENTEEN

Bar. Roe and Daniella.

Roe: Great.
Daniella: Wanna hear?
Roe: Sometime.
Daniella: Goes (she hums a trite melody).
Roe: Terrific.
Daniella: Sing it?
Roe: Needs accompaniment.
Daniella: A capella I'm used to.
Roe: I guess.
Daniella: Get a break.
Roe: Sure.
Daniella: Tough.
Roe: Life.
Daniella: Contacts.
Roe: Who ya know.
Daniella: Producers.
Roe: Yeah?
Daniella: No ears.
Roe: Know people.
Daniella: You do?
Roe: Sure.
Daniella: Favour?
Roe: Sure. George says hi.
Daniella: Okay?
Roe: Okay. Problem.
Daniella: Yeah.
Roe: On the lam.
Daniella: Taxes are taxes.
Roe: Theft.
Daniella: I know.

Roe: He make money?

Daniella: Sure.

Roe: Man makes money he's a criminal.

Daniella: Folks get angry.

Roe: They know?

Daniella: Little guy gotta pay.

Roe: Little guy's dumb.

Daniella: Sure. Like the song?

Roe: Pretty.

Daniella: Get a break, I'm made.

Roe: Wrote the President.

Daniella: George?

Roe: Me.

Daniella: Yeah?

Roe: Pardon.

Daniella: He say?

Roe: One letter.

Daniella: Do that?

Roe: Can.

Daniella: George know?

Roe: Sure. Remember?

Daniella: What?

Roe: Funeral.

Daniella: Oh, yeah.

Roe: Great man.

Daniella: Pity.

Roe: Right. On the plane. Somethin', eh?

Daniella: Sure.

Roe: Presidential invitation.

Daniella: Some plane.

Roe: Speed.

Daniella: Kiddin'.

Roe: Sad occasion.

Daniella: Own people killed him.

Roe: Crazy guy.
Daniella: Sure.
Roe: Remember I said.
Daniella: Yeah?
Roe: You talk.
Daniella: The President?
Roe: Why not?
Daniella: Listen to me?
Roe: His wife.
Daniella: Ex.
Roe: Intimate.
Daniella: And?
Roe: Know him.
Daniella: Sure.
Roe: Good man.
Daniella: Sometimes.
Roe: His heart.
Daniella: He's sick?
Roe: His soul.
Daniella: Got religion?
Roe: Who pays taxes?
Daniella: Everybody.
Roe: Losers. (Mobile sounds). Bob.
Bob Lund (off as for the rest of scene): Matt. Doin'?
Roe: Terrific. You?
Lund: Fine. Do for ya?
Roe: Remember Daniella?
Lund: Daniella?
Roe: Sure. George Marks.
Lund: Singing lady.
Roe: Got it.
Lund: Still warblin'?
Roe: Right here, Bob.
Lund: Don't say?

Roe: You know the President.
Lund: I do.
Roe: Worked in the White House.
Lund: Right.
Roe: Now, Daniella, she's thinkin'.
Daniella: Me?
Lund: She is?
Roe: A letter.
Daniella: I am?
Lund: To the President?
Roe: Sure.
Daniella: Minute.
Roe: George still on the lam.
Lund: Long time.
Daniella: Who is this?
Roe: White House counsel.
Daniella: Don't say.
Roe: You think, Bob?
Lund: Justice department.
Roe: Get in the way?
Lund: Sure.
Roe: Advice?
Daniella: Allergic to lawyers.
Lund: His wife.
Daniella: Ex.
Lund: Play the sentiment.
Roe: President sentimental?
Lund: Power is sentimental, Matt.
Roe: Hear that?
Daniella: I should sing?
Lund: Monroe.
Roe (sings): Happy birthday to you…(Laughs).
Lund: Legal guys.
Roe: Yeah?

Lund: Detail.

Roe: The devil.

Lund: Distract from the detail.

Roe: Hear that, Daniella?

Daniella: Am I a writer?

Lund: Flattery.

Roe: Get that, Daniella?

Daniella: Call him handsome?

Lund: Wealth is a mirror.

Roe: Yeah?

Lund: Power is a mirror.

Daniella: Say he's sexy?

Lund: Presidents are mirror gazers.

Roe: Get that, Daniella?

Lund: Show him the big man.

Daniella: I know him?

Lund: Magnanimous.

Daniella: He is?

Lund: You say.

Daniella: I do?

Roe: You do.

Lund: George is big.

Daniella: On the lam.

Roe: Worth?

Daniella: Knows?

Lund: Billions.

Roe: A billion. At least.

Daniella: Bribe?

Lund: Illegal.

Daniella: The law stops us?

Roe: The President.

Daniella: Honest?

Roe: Has to appear.

Daniella: Who'll know?

Lund: No need.

Daniella: No?

Lund: Get round a little boy. Give him candy.

Daniella: Candy?

Roe: Got it.

Daniella: Me?

Lund: Weaknesses.

Daniella: I'm a hooker?

Roe (laughs): No sex.

Daniella: A hooker without sex?

Lund: Wealth. Power.

Daniella: No bribe?

Roe: No.

Daniella: No sex?

Lund: No.

Daniella: Got me.

Roe: Big man. Generous. Magnanimous. Pardons the rich guy.

Daniella: The crook.

Lund: You know him.

Daniella: Crook.

Roe: Philanthropist.

Lund: Friend of mankind.

Roe: The poor.

Lund: The sick.

Roe: Culture.

Lund: Learning.

Roe: Benefactor.

Lund: Selfless.

Roe: Champion.

Lund: Good Samaritan.

Roe: Neighbour.

Lund: Messiah.

Roe: Saviour.

Lund: Redeemer.

Roe: Visionary.

Lund: Altruist.

Roe: Reformer.

Lund: Salt of the earth.

Roe: Saint.

Daniella: Saint?

Lund: Sure.

Roe: Why not?

Daniella: Saints evade taxes?

Roe: Everyone.

Lund: Human nature.

Daniella: President thinks?

Roe: Sure.

Lund: Write him.

Daniella: You?

Roe: Have.

Daniella: You say?

Roe (gets to his feet, recites): Dear Mr President, It has been my great honour and pleasure to know George Marks for many years as a personal friend. Never could a man have had a friend so loyal and generous. I know him to be a profoundly good man. His generosity to our people has been without bounds. In spite of his extraordinary misfortunes he has been a tireless worker for the good of mankind. The tragedy of heart disease which afflicted his own family led to him creating a foundation for research so that others may be spared the agony he knew. He has lost his home in the United States. And why? Because he broke some old laws. Was America made by obeying laws? He has made amends for his trifling mistakes. His endowments to education, culture, social programs and health amount to some hundred million dollars. In addition, I know him to be almost recklessly generous to individuals. He is a man of deep compassion. I believe it is now time to show to him the compassion he has shown to others. His suffering has been great. What good does his pain serve? Has the State no heart? He longs to be reunited with his family in the US. George Marks has made the world a better place. If all men were like him how fine a place our planet would be. He has been turned into a criminal because he transgressed a few outdated laws about trading with the so-called enemies of the US. The prosecutor's office refuses to discuss his case. Was America made by bureaucrats? I know you to be, like him, a man of great generosity and compassion. A great man. A great American. I appeal to you to release him from his suffering.

Lund: Genius.

Daniella: Reply?

Roe: Waiting.

Daniella: You write, I sign.

Lund: No, you.

Daniella: I sing.

Lund: Feminine touch.

Daniella: Yeah?

Roe: President likes women.

Daniella: Two letters?

Roe: Dozens.

Daniella: Who?

Lund: Professors.

Roe: Statesmen.

Lund: Writers.

Roe: Musicians.

Lund: Economists.

Roe: Scientists.

Daniella: Okay.

Roe: Good girl.

BLACKOUT

SCENE EIGHTEEN

Living-room. Marks alone, smoking cigar.

Prof Goodfriend (off): Dear Mr President, I write this letter to plead for clemency for George Marks who, as you know, has suffered exile for years. Can it be human to deny a man contact with his loved ones, to keep a man effectively imprisoned for alleged misdemeanours committed long ago? As Ambassador I got to know George Marks well and can tell you he was most highly regarded by the cream of society. His unstinting philanthropy and urbane manner have made him welcome in the most exclusive circles. He is a man of great honour and principle who has worked hard in the cause of world peace. Although I am unaware of the legal intricacies of this matter, I believe the only exit from this Kafkaesque impasse is for you to show him clemency. Your intervention may by the last chance of freedom for this unique man who has given so much to humanity. I call on you to review his case and use your power to end his cruel suffering.

Yours, Professor Harry Goodfriend, ex-Minister of Foreign Affairs, ex-Ambassador.

Marks paces.

Marks: Unstinting philanthropy (nods). Urbane manner (smooths his hair). Cream of society (puffs cigar and smiles). Unique man (nods).

Prof Armstrong (off) : Dear Mr President, I understand Mr George Marks is appealing to you for clemency. His case is a tragic one. As an ex-Minister of Justice I know only too well the plight of those who face the rigidity of the legal system. Law must have a heart. How painful it is to face the stone wall of cold justice which cannot hear and has no feelings. Mr Marks is an important private individual who has done much to promote inter-faith understanding. As a religious person myself I have the greatest regard for his spiritual qualities. He has won the respect and admiration of some of the wealthiest and most successful people in the world. I believe Mr Marks has paid his social debt to society and now is the time to treat him with the compassion he deserves.

Yours, Professor Clive Armstrong.

Marks (sits): Tragic. (draws on cigar). Rigidity of the legal system. (nods). No feelings. (draws on cigar). Spiritual qualities. (gets up, paces).

Oliver Ewart (off): Dear Mr President, I am writing on behalf of my good friend George Marks. My relationship with him goes back many years and I know him to be a man of the utmost discretion. He is a fine benefactor and his donations have secured a new wing for our oldest museum, cardiac and paediatric departments for two hospitals and a new library for our most prestigious university. In addition, of course, he has made multiple donations over many years. I think it is time to release him from the legal chains which have held him for nearly twenty years. Any wrongdoing, if any, has been expunged by his remarkable contribution to society as a whole. Can it be right to keep a man in exile for faults committed decades ago, as if he were no more than a common criminal? Set free to return to his homeland I'm sure he will continue to work for the welfare of the needy, as he has done all his life.

Yours, Oliver Ewart, ex-Minister of Health and Prime Minister.

Marks (contemplating himself in mirror): Fine benefactor. (Draws on cigar, nods). Remarkable contribution to society. (Laughs). Common criminal. (Scoffs).

Stella Baker (off): Dear Mr President, As a great admirer of yours I am appealing on behalf of the wonderful George Marks. I am just an entertainer and do not understand politics, but I know a good man when I meet one. (Marks sits. Extends legs. Draws on cigar). What has been done to George is just plain wrong. He has been forced to leave his country because of false allegations. I am not a lawyer but I know justice when I see it. Mr President, no one will look at the facts. He has been tried and convicted by the press. The prosecutors wanted to imprison him for life and why? Because he broke some old regulations about energy. I am just a singer and don't understand international relations but other people got away with it. He was accused of "trading with the enemy" but I know he has a good and giving heart and if he made a bit of money to help other people by bending the rules, is that so bad? A person is innocent until proven guilty and I can find no guilt in George, just a uniquely lovely man who likes to share his wealth with others. By doing so he has improved thousands of lives. Mr President, this is his last chance. I know you are a great man with a deep love of justice and mercy. Please do the right thing and set this good man free.

Respectfully, Stella Baker.

Marks (remains in same posture, draws on cigar and begins to chuckle, slowly becoming more hysterical until he is bent double with laughter. Leans back, wipes his eyes, shakes his head.) Is that so bad?

Robin Ingleson (off): Dear Mr President, As President of the University here I have got to know George Marks over the past few years. He has been inordinately generous to our institution and to many others which help our people. He makes no show of his philanthropy preferring to remain anonymous, a tribute to his modesty and self-effacing nature. We have a wide circle of friends in common including many highly successful businessmen among whom he is held in the highest regard. I believe it is a principle of justice that clemency is shown to those who seek to repay their debt to society. I believe George to have done so, many times over. Please use your power to grant him the right to return to his country and to live as a free and law-abiding citizen.

Sincerely, Professor Robin Ingleson, ex-Ambassador.

Marks: (Gets up. Looks in mirror. Smooths hair.) Modest and self-effacing. (Nods. Draws on cigar. Points index finger of right hand at his image.) Held in the highest regard. (He sits. Stretches. Smokes.)

Irene Berger (off): Dear Mr President, As you approach the end of your second term I would like to congratulate you on your extraordinary service to the people of the USA and the world. We have been truly blessed to have a man of such vision and high moral standards as the leader of the free world. All of us dream of being able to use our God-given abilities to help others. It is the most Godlike capacity to be able to do so, to be in the fortunate position to be able to renew life. As a woman of religion I believe it is humanity's highest calling. You are a man with a passion for justice and a dedication of heart to the causes of peace and human dignity. Soon, sadly, you will have less powers. I know when your Presidency is over you will go on with your work of healing a broken humanity and bringing solace to the suffering. After 20th January you will no longer have the power to grant clemency. It is a Godlike power and you have exercised it like a god. I am urging you, in these the final days of your magnificent administration, to use your God-like power one last time to end the appalling suffering of poor George Banks. I met him through his philanthropy and I know him to be a man filled with the desire to do good. God has seen fit to make him rich and who are we to question God's wisdom? His wealth has permitted George to behave like a god, to bring relief to suffering and to promote peace and understanding among humanity. He has always been willing to take a leadership role but never for his own gain. It is the good deed which attracts him not the publicity. He is a man who really cares. You can end his pain and suffering and help him to make up by making a better world. Released by your compassion, he can follow a new path, open a new life. The end of your term of office is a period for moral clarity, wider perspectives. You will no longer be in the political cross-hairs and only one question now faces you: will you help one more person, restore one more life, will you inspire George to do yet more good in the world ? If so, your action will bring good to humanity for many years ahead.

In admiration, Irene Berger, Chair of the International Committee of Remembrance.

Marks: (Gets up. Looks in mirror. Smiles broadly at himself. Momentarily his image is replaced by that of Bill Clinton- for theatre in the round, several images of Clinton should be projected. He staggers back a pace. Rubs his eyes. His image is restored. He smokes. Paces. Turns to inspect the mirror. Smiles at himself.) God-like power. (Nods). Leadership role. (Turns to the audience as if he going to address them. Assumes the demeanour and apes the gestures of an orator.) Filled with the desire to do good. (Puffs on the cigar).

Colin Morris (off): Dear Mr President, It is my honour to write to you as the most powerful man in the world. I have been most impressed by your compassion and the high moral standards you have shown throughout your time in office. I know you are aware of the desperate plight of George Banks, a man more sinned against than sinning. I have known him for many years as a highly successful businessman, greatly respected by the international business community. Also, as a philanthropist of extraordinary generosity, not only to our people but to the unfortunate amongst those with whom we are in conflict. He has endowed medical facilities for children and provided sports opportunities for young people. Might I add this has kept the terrorists who threaten us out of crucial areas. Whatever misdemeanours he may have committed, his slate is surely wiped clean by his charitable efforts. I call on you to exercise your power of forgiveness towards this excellent man.

Respectfully, Colin Morris, Founder of Morris Enterprises.

Marks: (Sits. Nods.) Greatly respected.

Daniella Marks (off): Dear Mr President, (Marks sits up and listens attentively) As a friend and admirer, I am writing on behalf of my ex-husband George Marks to ask you to end the cruel pain which has been inflicted on him and his family for nearly two decades. An innocent man punished because the press pursued him and the law was unwilling to listen to his case. Mr President, I tell you, there has never been a case like this in American history. He is a man with a good heart who has benefitted the lives of many by his selfless generosity. His reward has been exile from his country, his family and his friends. We have all suffered with him. Can it

Be right to punish a man's family in this way? It has been claimed he has broken a few rules about trading with this and that country. People break these rules all the time but only he has been accused. Ambitious lawyers see the opportunity to further their careers. Can we call this justice? I believe you know my ex-husband is a good man. I, who know him probably better than anyone have seen at close quarters the hard work he does on behalf of others with no concern for his own advantage. Do the right thing, Mr President, set this good man free to continue his work for the benefit of humanity.

Yours, Daniella Marks.

Marks: (Gets up. Looks in mirror.) Never been a case like this. (Nods). People break these rules all the time.

From off comes a cacophony of all the voices we have heard, contending with one another for attention, the volume rises and the competition tightens. Marks stands mid-stage, looking up, down, left and right, turning in circles, until the voices reach their crescendo and suddenly cease.

BLACKOUT

SCENE NINETEEN

Restaurant. Marks, Roe and Daniella.

Roe: Got it.

Marks: Free man.

Roe: Back to the States?

Daniella: Heard my new album?

Roe: No

Daniella: Should.

Roe: Sure, honey.

Marks: Civil case.

Roe: Fight it.

Marks: Hundred and seventy million fine is enough.

Roe: See the President's op-ed? (Produces copy of the New York Times).

Marks: See. (Reads).

Roe: Two law professors.

Marks: Uh-uh.

Roe: Classic.

Marks: Helpful.

Roe: Respectability always convinces.

Daniella: Need publicity.

Roe: Buy it.

Daniella: You've got money.

Roe: We've all got money.

Marks: All his advisers against.

Roe: Gotta go straight to the power.

Daniella: Need a hit.

Marks: You've had hits.

Daniella: Twenty years.

Roe: Justice department fulla liberals.

Marks: Else can he say?

Roe: Convinced him.

Marks: Flattered.

Daniella: You got a pardon, I need a hit.

Roe: Ask the President.

Marks and Roe laugh.

Marks: Give a million to the Democrats.

Roe: Or the Republicans.

Marks: Who's in power.

Roe: Money is money. Know there's a fellowship at Oxford in your name?

Marks (Sets aside paper, lights cigar): Don't say?

Roe: Respectability.

Daniella: Put a bit my way.

Marks: You're well regarded.

Roe: Little guy likes it.

Marks: Throw some crumbs.

Roe: Exactly.

Marks: Sports.

Roe: I know.

Marks: Hockey team. Best in the country. Cost me?

Roe: How much?

Marks: Coupla hundred thousand.

Roe: Peanuts.

Marks: Little guy's happy.

Daniella: Little guy needs entertainment.

Roe: Correct.

Marks: Deputy Attorney recommended?

Roe: Did.

Marks: Good guy.

Roe: The best.

Marks: Our people.

Roe: Crucial. Grateful.

Marks: Sure.

Daniella: Have to consult my angels.

Roe: Good idea.

Marks: Security used my offices worldwide.

Roe: Great. The oil too.

Marks: The secret is control.

Roe: Control means being secret.

Marks: Went public.

Roe: Sure.

Marks: Matters is beating the market.

Roe: Markets bad for profit.

Roe: You bet. Dictators, kleptocrats, oligarchs. Good for business.

Marks: Worst thing for business?

Roe: Yeah?

Marks: Democracy.

Roe: Little guy interfering.

Marks: He know?

Roe: Ignorance is good for him.

Daniella: Know how many vitamins I took today?

Roe: Surprise us.

Daniella: Thirty.

Marks: Feel better?

Daniella: My past life.

Roe: Yeah?

Daniella: Native American.

Marks: Get wiped out.

Roe and Marks laugh.

Daniella: In touch with nature.

Roe: Watch it.

Marks: Out of touch with business.

Daniella: Psychics say a hit is coming.

Roe: No kiddin'? Know what they say?

Marks: What?

Roe: You own Peru.

They laugh.

Marks: I do.

Roe: Gotta get the intelligence agencies.
Marks: Got 'em.
Roe: Warlords.
Marks: Them too.
Roe: Who ever invented democracy anyway?
Marks: Greeks.
Roe: Losers.
Daniella: Angels working for me.
Marks: Keep 'em busy.
Roe: Know what?
Marks: Yeah?
Roe: Need a President who'll shut down democracy.
Marks: Who?
Roe: Dunno.
Marks: Well-known.
Roe: Sure. Rich.
Marks: Yeah. Business not politics.
Roe: Business replaces politics.
Marks: Oil man.
Roe: Maybe. Stir up the rednecks.
Marks: Patriots.
Roe: Democracy? Bah. Nationalism.
Marks: Got it.
Roe: Our people. Land and blood.
Marks: Correct.
Roe: Daniella's native Americans. Backward.
Daniella: Hey, my past life.
Marks: Push those people aside.
Roe: Gotta.
Marks: The blacks.
Roe: Arabs.
Marks: Way behind.
Roe: Got a history?
Marks: Our history.

Roe: Correct.

Daniella: Hear my new song?

Marks: Sometime.

Roe: Got some vitamins to take?

Roe and Marks laugh.

Marks: World Economic Forum.

Roe: Yeah?

Marks: Get me there?

Roe: Why not?

Marks: Marshal on my tail.

Roe: Bodyguards. Gets near, you're away.

Marks: Guy been at it fourteen years.

Roe: Loser.

Marks: Pay him off?

Roe: Incorruptible.

Marks: No one.

Roe: You care? You steal Ceausescu's fortune, he counts his dollars.

Marks: Thought he was in control.

Roe: Wasn't?

Marks: Control the commodities. I bought at a fair price. Once I was sole provider, I was their pimp.

Roe: Whole country.

Marks: Worked for me.

Roe: Some payroll.

Marks: World on your payroll, that's business.

Daniella: Things to do.

Marks: More vitamins?

Roe: Talk to your angels?

They laugh.

Roe: So what's next?

Daniella: I need a hit.

Marks: Trade is neutral.

Roe: Correct.

Marks: Can't trade and have sympathies.

Roe: Got it.

Daniella: Be big again.

Roe: Doin' fine.

Marks: Make the world neutral.

Roe: Democracy, votes,blah, blah.

Daniella: Big concert.

Marks: China.

Roe: In there?

Marks: Gangsters.

Roe: Control the commodities.

Marks: State in the way. Democracy in the way in the US..
Am I a politician?

Roe: Are not.

Daniella: Big stars.

Marks: Clear the field for business.

Roe: Gotta.

Daniella: Relaunch.

Marks: Need a politician who'll destroy politics.

Roe: Who?

Marks: Take on China.

Roe: Yeah.

Marks: Billions to be had.

Roe: Locked out.

Marks: Think Bolivia.

Roe: Comibol?

Marks: Take the mines for the people. Who processes? Who
markets?

Roe: You.

Marks: Peters Brothers.

Roe: Nationalisation is good for business.

Marks: Way back. 1931. International Tin Agreement. Cut
production push up prices.

Roe: Good for business.

Marks: Peters broke the agreement.

Roe: What's an agreement for?

Marks: 1952 sold Santa Fe to Comibol.

Roe: Good deal?

Marks: They got the mine, Peters got minerals as collateral.

Roe: Genius.

Marks: They produced, Peters processed, marketed, financed.

Roe: Losers.

Daniella: Gotta consult my guru.

Roe: And your angels?

Marks: Your past life.

Daniella: See you guys.

Roe: Daniella?

Daniella: Yeah?

Roe: Don't forget the vitamins.

She goes.

Marks: Seventies, eighties. Lent the government money. Minerals as collateral.

Roe: Can't lose.

Marks: All over the world. Governments taking back resources for their people. We move in on processing, legal services, technical advice, marketing, capital. People get the hard work, we get rich.

Roe laughs.

Roe: Dumb governments.

Marks: Know what I learnt early?

Roe: Yeah?

Marks: Break the rules.

Roe: Rules are for losers.

Marks: You bet.

BLACKOUT